VIGNETTES FROM THE TWILIGHT OF LIFE

Vignettes from the Twilight of Life

Bruce Van Ness

To order additional copies of this book, contact:
Xlibris
844-714-8691
www.Xlibris.com
Orders@Xlibris.com
836609

PREFACE

His name was Afrin J. Heath, no relation to the decongestant or the candy bar, but distantly related to the Bayonne Heaths living in New Jersey. There was nothing he could do about that, but the Afrin part, that was different. Was God bored on that March day in 1945, or did he just have a mischievous streak and whisper it into his mother's ear? Or maybe, his parents just freaked when the head and shoulders popped out, and one of the nurses fainted with an "Oh my God!" Turns out she missed lunch, and her sugar dropped. Anyhow, when Afrin turned eleven, he rallied some courage and asked his parents about the name. "My friends have normal ones like John, and Pete. How come you called me Afrin? Could I have a normal one too?" "That was your mother's idea," his father said, dismissing any responsibility. "I don't know," she said defensively, shrugging her shoulders and glaring at her husband. She turned back to Afrin and smiled, holding his small hands comfortingly in her palms. "Mommy needed some medicine when you were born and said some silly things. All these years and we didn't know your name bothered you." She squeezed his hands gently. "We can fix that."

The next day his parents started calling him Jarvis. That was his middle name. Not much better, but a compromise chosen by his mother. His father originally wanted Jarhead, honoring the old man's service in the Marine Corp. "I know dad loves the service, but Jarhead?" Jarvis remarked after his mother explained why he had been blessed a second time with such an unusual name. Later in college when he repeated the story to friends he added, "I love my father, but he must have been smoking some awfully strong cigarettes."

Thirty-one years later his first name surprisingly got some recognition, though not in the way he would have imagined. In 1975, there was a new decongestant sitting on pharmacy shelves, and its name sounded strangely familiar.

"It only took three decades for you to be exonerated," he joked with his parents. "I'm famous. Just shove me in your nose and spray." A typical dry comment that marked his observation of life's little nuances.

Chapter One

"Another day on Driftwood Avenue," Jarvis grumbled schlepping into the kitchen to get his breakfast. It was one of those mornings he felt duty bound to question everything, including how the street got its name. "I've been living here all these years and still don't know why someone named the street Driftwood. There's not even a lake within five miles."

He scratched his belly out of habit and frowned at the aches that clenched the right side of his seventy-four year old body. "God, what's going to happen when I turn seventy-five. I'm just beginning to resign myself to the normal pains," he groaned, "and now these new ones. I must have slept all twisted up with my right arm curled underneath me. It'll go away. Maybe." He slowly rotated the affected shoulder to work out the kinks. His neck also hurt, but that was a fifty-year old military injury that flared up every now and again, especially with an impending change in the weather.

"Molly, wish you had hung around a few more years," Jarvis said peeking up at the ceiling. "You were good at patching things together. I could use some baling wire and duct tape. Probably better than the joints I have right now."

He clenched his forehead tightly as he began to ponder why he was having the frequent dreams which had unforgivingly been pursuing him since the beginning of the year. Usually at night, but sometimes they intruded upon the daydreams he had while napping after lunch. It was as if they had been wandering around all these years and then just decided to drop in and visit.

He cast about for the statement lawyers had used during his thirty-six years in Real Estate. *What was it again? Oh yea, "Time is of the essence."*

Hmm, maybe my time is drawing near, and I'm subconsciously taking inventory before splat, life's over, just like the spiders I smashed when Molly was alive. Jarvis chuckled. He could still hear his wife's phobic screaming if he tried hard enough. *Better be on my best behavior, or is it too late for that? The line is moving slow, but inevitably forward "your turn Mr. Heath."* He shook his head drolly and matted down some defiant hairs he noticed in the glass of the cabinet door. *"Yep, no missteps now or pfft. You take the slide over there mister. I never did like the heat."*

Jarvis turned on the coffee maker and frowned. "I need this to wake up." During the night, a nostalgic infatuation had meddled with his sleep, leaving him tired and baffled. *Why this particular one?* There were at least three other relationships he deemed more significant. Four if he exaggerated. He finally shrugged it off as nothing more than a random roll of the die.

When he was in seventh grade, he liked the skinny girl who sat three rows in front of him. "I am not in love with her," he argued with the two prickly twerps he called friends. "That would be just crazy. But she's friendly, and I like her." He purposely hid the real reason for his affection. She was smart. Seventh grade boys weren't supposed to like girls who were smart.

Three weeks later however, Jarvis abruptly awakened one morning, aghast that he could ever have been so mesmerized with her. "I mean, she's smart, wears glasses, and runs funny. How stupid can I be?" However, over the long, hot summer, hormones ravaged that skinny body, and when she returned to school in the fall, Jarvis was mostly dumbfounded, yet strangely affected by how her body moved. Flat shirts now swelled out in the front, the glasses were missing, and her butt wiggled from side to side when she walked. Yikes. She had become pretty and smart.

Jarvis figured spending more than half his life as a realtor made him a quasi-expert on love. In the early years, couples often arrived at the office locked arm in arm, and gushing excitement about buying a home. However, after spending two to three hours on the road, some of them would leave like they were two, steely magnets, north and south poles repelling each other. "It didn't have a man-cave. I want four bedrooms. But we only have two children! Not enough countertops in the kitchen. But you don't cook! I will if I have enough countertops. It's too much property to mow. But I want more property. Then you mow the grass!"

In the late nineties, with the advent of Real Estate advertising online, Jarvis presumed any dissension would be resolved before arriving in the office. He reasoned that would be the pragmatic, and for him, headache free provision of the new technology.

So ideally, they would come in armed with the listings they wanted to see and prepared to make an offer on which ever one appealed to their lofty desires. Yet some buyers still couldn't agree to leave discriminating opinions at the door and behaved more like territorial combatants than a couple in love. "I like the openness of the downstairs. Too open for my taste! I don't like the color of the living room. I love it!" And what always killed Jarvis were the soon to be married ones who threw their hands up, and said, "I'm done," before they had even said "I do."

"Probably a good thing," Jarvis mused, and then, "It's all about give and take ladies and gentlemen. Give and take." Course for some couples, putting that into practice, was tantamount to having a noose slipped around their necks.

The kitchen didn't seem any bigger to Jarvis even with his beloved Molly gone. Matter of fact, there were days it felt too small with unwashed bowls and pans cluttering the counters. They seemed to purposely pile up to remind him he was alone and would have to be the one to clean them.

Molly would never have allowed the mess to happen. She was irritatingly neat, and obsessive-compulsive, about everything being in its place. She would have no problem chiding him about the plate and cup he just put in the sink.

"Two feet to your left, and you could have deposited them in the dishwasher. Even the kids have learned that lesson."

"Yes Dear," he would dutifully say, not to be condescending or anything, but just to sound contrite enough for his ritualistic misdeed. Strange, but he missed that repartee with her. Upon occasion, he would intentionally disobey one of her wifely requests, and smother the woman with all the apologetic wiles of a passionately hungry man, pressing up against her butt, and whispering, "I'm sorry. What can I do to make it up to you?" Sometimes his carnal plan actually worked.

But since Molly died, he mostly just washed, and rinsed his stuff in the sink, and let them dry. Besides, it would probably take him a whole week to fill the washer, and by that time, all the glop would be adhered like glue.

Jarvis hitched up his drooping briefs and growled with frustration at the persistent twinge in his shoulder. Then he surveyed the cereal and dry fruit in the cabinet above his head which coaxed a smirk to defiantly appear. Big decision to make. If boxes could be telltale signs of old age, these certainly would be, Bran, Cornflakes, prunes and raisins. "God, I'm surprised I don't have diarrhea."

He got the flakes and raisins down and poured them into a bowl. Several shots of milk, and he was set. Molly had always stressed to him how important it was to keep the pipes clean. "Don't want to get them clogged again."

"Hmm, she was right about that." He remembered the appendicitis, the surgery, and the recovery afterward when he was forty-three. Constipated because of the pain medicine. Poop the size of softballs. He didn't know if the pain was worse, or the anxiety, and humiliation that he couldn't take a dump, and needed an enema.

He scuffed back into the living room and set the bowl down on the tray table so he could watch the TV and eat. A real luxury because Molly would never have let him do that. He smiled. Whenever she went away to babysit the grandkids for a few days, he would cheat almost the whole time.

Jarvis found the remote and searched for the local news. He routinely watched it to get the day's weather, and for the brunette who usually did the traffic report. She could just stand there, not saying anything, and he would wallow in her beauty. "I may be seventy-four, but I can still recognize fine art when I see it. Crap. It's that fat guy again, but she'll be back tomorrow."

CHAPTER TWO

Jarvis was usually not one to procrastinate and could not understand why some people seemed content to let things go until the last minute. "Still be there in the morning. Rather tackle it now and get it done," was his mantra.

However he did make a few exceptions to the rule and going to the dentist was one of them. Normally it had taken a nagging reminder from Molly for him to make an appointment to have his teeth checked, but this time it was the throbbing pain on the right side of his mouth.

A dentist appointment this early in the morning is such a wonderful way to start the day, Jarvis thought flippantly. Just the anticipation makes my heartbeat faster and my palms sweat. But at least it will be out of the way.

Nothing like hearing the shrill sound of a drill as it digs into your tooth. I get tense just listening to someone else being worked on. He could still hear the dentist saying, "Oh, but Mr. Heath, the Novocain should prevent any discomfort, and if by some chance there is a little pain, just let me know." *Love to doc, just watch how deeply my fingers press into the arms of the chair. Not great for blood pressure either. But so far, so good. Probably take half a day for the numbness to wear off. I love liquids dribbling out of my mouth.*

"It's just a little cavity," the dentist said at the beginning. "Still give you some local." The man was wearing glasses, "So I can see better."

I'd feel better if you didn't need any glasses while drilling in my mouth. However, always been impressed that no one has punctured my tongue. Damn thing moves all over the place. And please don't tell your assistant a joke. Tough laughing with all this crap in my mouth.

"Uh!" Jarvis moaned. *Now that hurt!*

"Sorry Mr. Heath. I can give you more medicine if you want, but there's just a little more to do."

"Uh huh. Ohh!" Jarvis's venomous stare and white knuckled grip tacitly screamed his ire and pain.

"Sorry. A little bit more. Okay, I'm done."

That Union General, hmm, Sherman, said "War is hell. It certainly is, but he should have sat in a dentist chair. Words he could not speak out loud because the sucky thing and a thin metal instrument with a mirror on the end were now poking around in his mouth.

"Looks good. See, it was just a small cavity," the dentist announced.

A small cavity?! I thought you were sinking a damn well!

The man smiled benevolently at Jarvis. "Give me some amalgam and I'll fill this," he directed his assistant.

Why don't you sit your ass down in this chair and let me drill for a few minutes, Jarvis thought with bridled annoyance. But he couldn't blame the dentist entirely. He hated the needle and burning medicine as much as the actual drilling and had asked for as little of the anesthetic to be used as possible. *I'm a tough guy. Perhaps not as tough as I used to be.*

"Next time I'll give you more Novocain Mr. Heath."

What next time? I'm never coming back here.

"I'll write you a script for some pain pills. By tomorrow you should be feeling better." The dentist nodded at him reassuringly.

Jarvis tried to smile sarcastically.

Fifteen minutes later he was in a pharmacy pick-up line. He tried to speak, but his jaw still felt like a catcher's mitt, and all that came out was a spray of saliva. *Going to take one of these when I get home. The dentist said it would lessen the pain and help me get some rest.* Jarvis paused and tried to scrunch his mouth in contemplation. *Jeez, I feel like I've been in a workout. My nerves are shot, ha ha, and I have a headache.*

Back at the house, he swallowed one of the tablets, taking some pudding with it so he wouldn't get nauseous. His mother taught him that trick. Then he lay on his lounger and closed his eyes. "Sleep will come," he told himself.

His mother had been the cog that kept everything running smoothly in the family. She made sure his father was happy, at least within the four walls of the house, and if he did come home disgruntled, she was the palliative for his distemper. *High school sweethearts, like many couples back in those days,* Jarvis presumed. *That was before the big war that came after the one that was supposed to end all wars. Dad volunteering for the Marine Corp, and staying in the service to visit Korea on the behest of Uncle Sam. Each time it elicited a few tears from mom, but she found the courage, and mustered up.*

Besides the cooking and cleaning around the house, she helped with food drives, PTA, and was his cheerleader during little league games. They weren't as close as he would have liked because he didn't want to be tagged as a momma's boy. Too many of his classmates were hardened military brats and that would have been tough to live down. But one day she insisted he come with her to visit a local cemetery. He was nine at the time, and not too keen about places where the dead were buried.

"Jarvis, time for you to learn the truth," his mother mysteriously said as he followed her down one of the paths. In the car she had been quiet and scarily sad. *Maybe she doesn't like cemeteries either,* Jarvis thought. He noticed a swirl of wind tossing up strands of her long blond hair, and from his height, the firm calves that flexed with each stride. He had heard his father say he was blessed to have such a pretty wife. His mother was walking fast, like she wanted to get this whole experience over with, and his short legs had to double time. "We're going over there," she said pointing to his left. They trooped past a few unadorned graves before stopping before one with a headstone engraved "Cyndi L Heath 1943-1948."

Jarvis looked up at his mom, his face wrinkled in confusion. "This person has the same last name I do."

"Yes, she does," his mother said, like she was hurting somewhere and didn't want him to see her pain. She knelt down and started pulling out some of the weeds and grass. "Did you know mommy was unhappy yesterday and today?"

"Uh huh," Jarvis said, sure they were the right words to say. "You had droopy eyes."

"Yes, I had droopy eyes." She smiled through tears and rubbed his back. "Did you know you had a sister?"

"I think so."

"Cyndi was two years older than you. When she was five..."

"I was three?" he interrupted, proudly counting in his head.

"Yes, you were three. She got very sick and was admitted to the hospital." His mom dabbed her wet eyes and cheeks.

He glanced at the headstone again, and then back at his mother. This time there were tears in his own eyes. "Did she die?"

A heavy sigh greeted him. "Yes Jarvis, that is what happened. Your daddy and I loved her so much." Her shoulders shook as unforgiving sobs escaped."

Jarvis nudged closer and draped his arm around her. He had never seen her upset this way and it frightened him a little bit. "I'm sorry mommy. Don't cry," he murmured.

"You going to be mommy's big soldier today?"

His bottom lip quivered. "Okay." He looked back at the name. "How come I don't remember her very well?"

"You were so young and probably don't remember much."

"Is daddy sad?"

"Yes, he is, but sometimes big men don't like to show they're sad."

"Oh." Jarvis looked inquiringly at her. "Can we talk about something happy?"

"I would like that, Jarvis. You know daddy has a garden full of tomatoes, and some animal has been eating them. The other day your father came into the house and said, "You're not going to believe this, but I just saw a squirrel squatting on one of the fence posts and nibbling a tomato. It stopped, looked over at me, orange pulp around its mouth, put the tomato down like he felt guilty and then bounded off. If I hadn't seen it, I wouldn't have believed it."

"That's a good one mommy," Jarvis said between giggles. "I feel better. Do you feel better?"

"Much," his mother said.

CHAPTER THREE

When the scratches of sunlight finally woke Jarvis up, he rolled over and rubbed his left hip and knee. "Going to rain," he groaned, and then, "I tried to live healthy all my life, and this is how my body thanks me?" He scowled, angry with the stabbing pain besieging his joints. "Have to be like this as soon as I wake up?" he complained to some contentious spirit. The doctor said it was arthritis, and there was little he could do besides the medicine he was already taking. "Doubt that," Jarvis grumbled when he left the office. "Probably graduated the bottom of his class."

He peered at the clock on the dresser and frowned. *Must have dozed off. Know my days are emptier than they used to be, but mornings are still the best part.* He counted to three, and swung his legs around, so the momentum pulled him into an upright position. "Hard part done," he remarked. "Thank God, once I start moving, the pain practically disappears." He paused and shook his head reprovingly. "Guess I should be lucky the heart and brain haven't given me much trouble, yet." He stood up, taking his first reluctant steps like an infantryman having to go on a five-mile march. "Forward."

Forty-five minutes later he plopped down in the lounge chair to watch TV. No channel surfing, just ceding his attention to whichever program appeared on the screen. He had slept late, so his news show was over. No traffic lady today and instead, some renowned psychologist Jarvis never heard of was speaking to a Friday morning audience. He came across as arrogant and feigning sincerity. "What are the reasons you get out of bed in the morning, and do they make you glad?"

It was like a test and Jarvis had a pat answer. "I get out of bed to pee, and I am really happy about that. Matter of fact, I make it a practice to pee in the middle of the night too. So, I guess I should be twice as happy. Ah, now my day is complete. Idiot." He sighed and turned off the television. "Not feeling myself today. Must have been the late night, the drinks, and the two women in the hot tub." The foolish conjecture solicited a derisive smirk.

His eyes strayed around the room, haphazardly, without hope of finding something that would remedy the nascent malaise. "Just something to divert me for a little while," Jarvis said.

"Maybe I can start reading one of those books on the shelf. Finish it before I die. Molly will be so proud of me. Would be so proud," he corrected. "What's that one, Anna Karenina? A love story, isn't it? She has an affair, and then commits suicide?" Jarvis's wrinkled brow showcasing his half-hearted enthusiasm. *No, I think I'll leave that one alone. Besides, looks awfully thick. Though Molly did say it was one of her favorites by Tolstoy.* He chuckled. *I'd kid her by saying Toetoy. I guess after the third time, it isn't very funny.*

Shortly after his wife died, Jarvis began to occasionally hear the distant echo of old conversations in the empty house. He realized it was only his imagination, but sometimes he almost expected Molly to walk in on him, the lilac scent of her cleansing the stale air, and coaxing old memories to come out from hiding. Sometimes he would chat with her as if she was right there in the room, or at least, with the presumption she was bending down from above to hear him.

They had been married so long he could often anticipate what she would say. And if her opinion was different than his own, it benefited him to keep his mouth shut. Sometimes however, he could be very stupid.

It did seem foolish those first few weeks to converse with Molly when she was no longer around, but after a while it seemed only natural. He spoke with his daughter Shelly to get her take on their, spirited dialog, and she just shrugged her shoulders and said it was harmless. "You and mom were so close."

However, when he joked about it with one of his friends, he was told such behavior could indicate the onset of dementia, and maybe he should follow up with a neurologist. *Just what I need, another doctor.* It worried him for about two minutes. *Ah, hell. I've always been demented. Never worried about it before. Usually ignore any gratuitous advice anyway.*

Jarvis took out his cell phone to check for messages and skim the number of new emails. He deleted them every night, and silenced the ringer, figuring if something was important, Michael, and Shelly knew where to find him.

"Ya know baby," he murmured, glancing toward the ceiling, "for the longest time I kept your voice on the answering machine we used for the landline. Sounds crazy, but I'd call our number several times a week just to hear you. His eyes glazed with self-indulgent sadness. *Allowed to feel sorry for myself once in a while, huh?*

"Damn. I completely forgot." Jarvis groaned, upon seeing the date niched into the corner of the home screen. He hung his head in shame, and then looking up pensively, confessed, "Sorry Molly. Our anniversary. Promised you I'd always remember." He rested his chin on his opened hand, remorseful, and concerned that after two years, he already had forgotten their special day. "Dementia? Nah."

Leaning his head on the back of the chair, he spied a treasured memento on the mantle, and smiled. It beckoned forth memories that provided a salve to the wounds Molly's passing still left behind. It was a day that could compete in importance to the one when they took their vows. His own conscience spurring him to "find the balls!" and ask her.

He and Molly had been living together for seven months, soaking in the sultry heat of their love. Idiosyncrasies like his compulsion to have all the clocks set ten minutes fast because it was better to be early than late. And the fact that she loved Rock and Roll, and he loved Country had not displaced the passion they felt for each other. Jarvis could feel his heart begin to pound just a little bit faster when he thought about that impromptu moment when he finally took the leap of faith.

They had made plans to go to the beach for a few days, and that was where he would surprise her. But Jarvis wanted to do it in a novel way, something that would have been worthy of a you tube video in today's world. It had been difficult containing his excitement, although it was tempered by the splash of fear that she'd say no. The same trepidation which had made him hesitant for so long.

Welling up his courage, he had bought a one and a half carat ring, which provided the incentive to ask her. "Frugal, even back then," Jarvis admitted. He carried the little red box with him every day, so he would be prepared for any unique, impromptu moment. And when the time appeared right, wham.

Maybe a few drinks first, and then, in the middle of me doing some karaoke, substituting a stanza, "Oh Molly, I need you. I love you. Won't you be mine... forever?" "How corny that would have been," Jarvis mumbled, wincing.

He remembered her guiding him into one of those beach front stores loaded with all sorts of knickknacks, towels, swimming gear, and shirts with smart-ass saying on them. Molly had gone off to look at bathing suits, leaving him time to wander aimlessly around a store he would never have stepped foot in if he was alone.

Hey, this is clever, he thought, carefully picking up two shells hinged together in the back, with googly eyes glued to the top shell, and tiny sandals attached to the bottom like feet. "Looks like a clam. Hmm."

He opened the mouth to see how much room was inside. "Yea, this will do," he said, congratulating himself on the find. "Molly, over here!" he shouted, probably too loudly, like a small kid excitedly nudging his first toad, and waiting for it to hop.

"What is it, Jarvis?" she asked scurrying over, a tone of quizzical concern in her voice. "You alright?"

"Fine."

"But you called me like there was something wrong."

"Just exuberance. Look at this clam. Isn't it neat?"

"Neat? A new vocabulary word? And this is what you want me to look at," she said glancing questionably at him, and picking up the beachy handicraft. "Does the mouth open? Is a tongue going to spring out, and scare me?"

"No, nothing like that." he said, conjuring some dark and dreary movie scenes to keep from grinning.

She lifted the top shell and gasped. Her face paled, and her hand visibly shook. "Oh Jarvis," she whispered, putting the clam down, and holding the little red box in her hand. "Is this...?"

Jarvis got down on one knee. "Will you..." he started nervously.

"You bum," Molly interrupted, and then, "Oh my God, yes. A million times yes!" Tears began to slide down her cheeks as she threw her arms around him.

"You're really not a bum," she whispered guiltily into his ear.

"I know," he replied softly, no longer wanting to suppress the crescent grin exposing his own happiness. "Now how about opening up the box."

CHAPTER FOUR

Two days every week, Jarvis volunteered to help deliver hot meals to people who were unable to cook their own, or in many instances, just couldn't afford the high prices at the store. The deliveries helped carry them through the month. He was gratified to do a little something that made their lives easier.

Sadly, he noticed many of the individuals were younger than him and often sick. This encouraged moments of thankfulness for his own health. Sure, he had high blood pressure and complained about the aches and pains that greeted him every morning, but they were nothing more than the imposition of getting older. "Like getting a bill at the end of the month if ya run a toll. Eventually it'll catch up with you." he explained to his male friends.

Today, the atmosphere in the delivery van seemed thick with apprehension. *We've been sitting at this stop for ten seconds, and no cars,* Jarvis thought looking over at the woman behind the wheel. "Quiet today. Uh, you okay?" he asked.

Kathy Mason glanced over, and shrugged her shoulders, as if he was supposed to guess whether she was having a good or bad day.

Usually each of them contributed to conversations about the children, news commentaries and anything else that transfixed their attention.

"Think we've solved all the world's problems right here in this van," Jarvis would tease. Sometimes they used each other as pressure valves to relieve daily annoyances and stresses that emerged from time to time. So, it seemed peculiar to him that for the past thirty minutes Kathy seemed oblivious of her passenger and had missed one of their turns. It appeared that something wasn't right.

She was a single mom with two children. Serious, but not obsessed about anything. However, Jarvis did feel rewarded whenever he could break through her pensive exterior and stir up some laughter. She was also taking online classes in business, or something like that. *It sounds like she has to make time in her schedule to breathe*, he had mused flippantly a few weeks back.

Kathy glanced at him with her lips pressed firmly together, and the sad eyes of someone lost and confused. And then, as if on cue, words began to burst from her like a dam collapsing, and she was helpless to stop the torrential flow that followed. Jarvis checked the sideview mirror, but there was no vehicle behind them.

"He's in jail," she blurted.

"In jail? Who?"

"My ex. Three months behind with child support. It's only four hundred dollars a month, and he won't pay it. Not even for his own children! He said if the money went directly to the kids, he would pay it, but it comes to me." She rolled her eyes. "They're only six and seven. Is he an idiot! He claims I spend most of it on beauty products and other stuff for myself! Is the food just for me? Do I wear the food? Do I look like I use all kinds of cosmetics? Huh?"

"Uh, no," Jarvis sputtered, hoping it wasn't a trick question. He remembered dating someone who normally spent forty-five minutes to an hour fixing herself up in the morning. She got sick and didn't wear any makeup. *Thank God she couldn't read my mind*, he had thought after visiting her.

"Then he says I'm bringing men home," Kathy continued, "and making out with them in front of the boys! I don't have the time or energy to see anybody. I'm trying to put myself through school, take care of the kids, and work this job, which doesn't pay very much. I count on his money for meals."

A horn beeped behind them. "Oh, go to hell," she growled, jerking the van across the intersection and sliding it next to the curb. "And the irony, I spend my days taking meals to people when I could use them myself." She stopped for a moment and grimaced as if in pain. Her hands were trembling.

"Trying to calm herself," Jarvis thought with wary anticipation. After all these years, he presumed he would have figured women out. Foolish idea.

Even to the end, his Molly gagged him with some of her responses." Too much testosterone, and not enough estrogen," she would say.

"And what a wonderful legal system we have," Kathy wailed. "First his wages are garnished, and then his driver's license is suspended. Now he can't get to work because his driving privileges have been taken away. So, what does the brilliant judge do, puts him in jail until he pays the child support which is in arrears! But he's not working! So where is the money supposed to come from? Ahh!"

"Oh my God, the poor girl. I want to help her, but what can I do or say?" Jarvis pondered the situation with an almost flailing desperation, like it was one of his grandkids brandishing their rage and needing his understanding and support. *I never saw her like this. Damn, I feel so useless.* He apparently was not very good at hiding his distraught, because when Kathy peeked over at him, the implacable anger etched on her face abruptly gave way to self-conscious shame, and contrition.

"Oh, I'm so sorry Jarvis. I should never have blasted you with my problems. I'm just so," she hesitated before continuing, "pissed off."

"Hey, I'm not in your shoes, but I can understand why you would be, pissed," Jarvis said. "Matter of fact, I've used that word a few times myself."

Kathy chuckled, and then exposed her repentant demeanor with an embarrassed smile. "I apologize again," she said.

"No problem, really," Jarvis replied, attempting to wave down her twinge of regret. "I'm a volunteer. I help deliver meals. Sometimes I do a little counseling on the side. But for this, I do charge a small fee."

"You're a nut, Jarvis."

"I'm seventy-four years old. I'm allowed to be a nut." And then a bravura of inspiration. "Uh, Kathy, acting on that nutty accusation, I was wondering, when we're done, how about lunch. If you have nothing against being seen in public with an old guy like me. I'll treat."

"Now, you're not hitting on me, are you?" she jested.

Jarvis grinned. "I'm harmless."

"I've heard those words before, but I could use the company. Let's finish up this route mister."

Back home, after the meal, Jarvis was resting in the recliner with his hands clasped behind his head. Evening seemed to have come early because the shades were drawn to keep out the heat, and the room was dim. "Every day is like romp through Adventureland," he kidded Kathy at lunch. "And I will tell you, at my age, it starts with just getting out of bed." She dutifully giggled at the analogy.

"In my world with the boys, most days are like Frontierland." She replied. It elicited a benevolently, smirky response from him, after which Kathy punctuated the silence with an ambiguous titter. "The other day I saw an advertisement for a parttime model at some art studio. It paid thirty dollars an hour. I was considering it until I read the small print. The individual is expected to sit naked in front of the class for at least a couple of the sessions. No way is this body sitting naked in front of anyone."

Jarvis belly laughed so deeply he had to hold his sides to lessen the pain, and then sputtered, "Wonder if they'd like this saggy, old body?" They both convulsed until their aching chests forced them to stop.

Jarvis pawed his chin distractedly. *Hmm, forgot to shave. Not only old, but beastly looking too.*

Hope I cheered Kathy up for a little while. Did have her laughing a few times. That was good. Made both of us feel better." He squinted purposelessly around the room until he saw the wedding picture on the side wall. "Molly was so beautiful," he murmured, "Of course there's me, with part of my shirt hanging out. I look so... unkempt. "Appearances aren't everything," she would tease. "I married you anyway."

Jarvis glanced upward. If you were peeking down a while ago baby, you would have been proud of me. I not only paid for the meal, but I convinced the young lady to take a check for one hundred dollars. Not much, but it should help toward bills. Told her to call me if she needs someone to pound on. Not literally, but she got what I meant.

He closed his eyes and allowed vagabonds of nostalgia to trespass in and out of his rumination. In one of them, Pastor Dennis was looking down from the pulpit at the congregation. With his youthful countenance, he looked like he was going to give a valedictorian speech rather than preach. It was the third in a series of sermons on BLTs, not bacon, lettuce and tomato he joked, but believing, loving and being thankful for God's gifts.

"So, what are you thankful for," Pastor Dennis asked near the conclusion of the service. He looked at the congregation with eagerness and anticipation. "Nothing to fear. We're all brothers and sisters in Christ.

"My children," a woman shouted out.

"My dog," said a man who had recently lost his wife.

Molly is glancing over here, wanting me to say something. I can feel her eyes, Jarvis thought. *Course my mind is blank.*

"Uh, three strikes," he blurted, as the idea suddenly swerved into his head. Immediately it was like a hundred needles pricking him as everyone in the sanctuary stared in his direction for an explanation. "I was engaged three times. I swung for the fence with the first two and missed the ball. Course my luck changed when I met Molly. We got engaged and I hit a homerun." There was a flattering "awe" echoing in Jarvis's ears. Molly grabbed his hand and gave him a kiss on the cheek. She found a better way to thank him when they got home.

CHAPTER FIVE

Sometimes Jarvis felt like he was hibernating in a cave because so much time was spent sitting in the living room. He would go out for his volunteering, and do some weekly shopping, but it did not compare to the hours spent at the Realty office or on the road with clients. When he opened the door to retirement, Molly was there to save him from the hapless monotony he feared might swallow his happiness. *I don't play golf. I fish when I can. Mow the lawn. Yea, that'll kill the boredom.* But not to fear, his wife had a list of home projects, suggestions for community service and vacations they had never taken. However, now she was gone, and some days it was a struggle to find that inner peace, and joy.

The fishing he liked to do was becoming complicated on account of the tremor he was developing in his hands, and this made it difficult to tie lures or bait hooks. Michael had promised to take him, but the last two times he visited, it was, "Next time dad. I'll put it on my calendar."

"Next time? Must think I have nine lives?" Jarvis quipped sarcastically. He turned the sound off on the television and tried to read the actors' lips. It was supposed to stimulate his brain according to some medical study. "This is ridiculous," he muttered. "Forgot my glasses, and from here every mouth looks like it's puckered for a kiss. Maybe if I was deaf, reading lips would come in handy. I'll take my chances."

He rubbed his chin in sentimental reflection as a smile crept across his face. "Molly swore I already was deaf to some degree. Something men develop when they get married. What did she call it, Spousal Hearing Impairment Theory or SHIT for short." He shook his head in flippant admiration. "She could be quite the smart-ass sometimes."

His glasses were in the kitchen, but Jarvis felt too lazy to get them.

So he called out in his best British accent, "Dyson old man, would you retrieve my glasses," as if there was a butler who would go into the kitchen and fetch them. "Thank God, I haven't lost my sense of humor," Jarvis mused.

He flashed his eyes around the room crimping his brows to see better. The doctor said he had cataracts, worse on the left, and would need surgery. However, the idea of someone poking around in his eyeballs sounded too scary. His sight wasn't so bad that he couldn't take in all the pastels, familiar knick-knacks, and various photographs of the family. *Yep, it has a real comfortable feel to it,* he thought contentedly. *Someday, when I die, I'd be happy to be buried right here, by the oak in the back yard. I'll start digging the hole right now.*

But he knew his place was beside his wife, and she was two hours away in a family plot bought many years before. *How morbid is that?* Jarvis thought. *Anticipating death. But not worse than the sign on the Administrator's desk at the cemetery,* "This is a cash and carry operation. You give us the cash, and we'll carry you in." It always elicited a charitable snicker.

Lately, when it was quiet like this, and he was still awake, old memories that had not drifted permanently away, would bob around gently in his head. Many of them endearing scenes of laughter, love and tears that only family and a wife of thirty-nine years could provide. If there was a God, and Jarvis believed there was, the omnipotent Being had been very good to him.

Molly had an extraordinary ability to recall childhood experiences, as if they were apples on a tree which just needed picking, remembering details he would have long since forgotten. Although she did have the advantage of being an English teacher, and every year she practiced learning about a hundred new names. It was like Pilates for the mind. Molly claimed to remember her fifth birthday party because her cousin Billy was having a tantrum, and when his mother picked him up, he kicked the cake off the table. She also liked to tease him about the first boy she kissed. She was eight, and his name was Robert.

Jarvis had dutifully chuckled, and asked, "You trying to get me jealous?"

"Just letting you know there are other men out there," she returned with a mischievous smile. "You remember your first kiss?"

"Mine? Let's see." and with much squinching of his eyes and mouth, Jarvis eventually snagged the moment from the entrails of his reminisces.

Her name was Diane, and she was the little girl who lived across the street growing up.

He believed it was Valentine's Day, nineteen fifty-six, when she darted up to him as he got off the school bus. "Jarvis, I have this for you," and pulled a red envelope from beneath her coat. "And this too," she said, giving a quick peck to his cheek. It was a tie who was more embarrassed. The kiss would be the only one he ever got from her.

Since there was no sound and a picture he could barely see, Jarvis reached for the remote and turned the television off. Then he squirmed his butt around until he was comfortable and shut his eyes. Two days earlier, he had been eating eggs that he fried over easy, and just staring blankly out the kitchen window, when images from the old neighborhood plopped into his head. *The Flynns? Why the Flynns?* he asked himself. They were an odd couple who lived where the street in his old neighborhood curved north toward Ionia Park. *They must be dead by now, or they'd be at least a hundred and fifty years old.*

The gossip from the adults suggested they were brother and sister and participated in some incestuous behavior. Of course, back then, he had no idea what incestuous meant, and was afraid to ask his parents. Admitting he overheard their adult conversation, even accidently, was tantamount to offering up a guilty plea and grounds for imprisonment in his room. But apparently whatever the Flynns were doing in their home guaranteed they were going straight to hell.

All the neighborhood kids pedaled faster on their bikes, or ran, not walked whenever they passed the house. Mrs. Flynn would sit on her porch and rock in an old green chair watching the street like a sentry, and dutifully report any misbehavior to parents. She had wild, white hair that stuck out at all kinds of angles, and always wore bright red lipstick.

Mr. Flynn had gray and white eyebrows that connected across the bridge of his nose, and if he ever got lockjaw, he could probably shove food through the gaps between some of his teeth.

In their backyard was this tiny greenhouse where the Flynns stacked bags of garbage until they piled above the windowsill. Then the couple would make their ritualistically trips to the dump, the stench of the fly infested contents warning the neighbors the old blue pickup was coming down the street. Jarvis chuckled. His mother would run around the house closing windows when she smelled it coming.

Every Halloween the Flynn house was shrouded in eerie blackness, without a flicker of light to dispel the rumor that they were nocturnal creatures who feasted upon little boys and girls. Ghoulish howls, and hair-raising screams stoked the imagination that another foolish trick or treater had met his or her demise.

Jarvis folded his arms behind his head and puffed his cheeks in and out like a blowfish. No particular reason. Just waiting patiently for the Flynns to fade away, and with them, some of the blemished beliefs of his childhood. But lying in wait was a nostalgic peek at the summer he turned thirteen and got his first job. *"So proud of myself until I found out exactly what I would be doing."* he thought, although now with a self-deprecating humor. *"I never felt so red faced. Still can't believe how much of a dimwit I was."*

Back then, the circus arrived in town every summer for three days of Big Top performances, and midway entertainment. They always needed temporary help, and Jarvis was one of the first individuals in line.

"We could use you to help with cleanup," a skinny man said while balancing his chair against the tent pole behind him. The odor of cigarette smoke and heavy sweat doubtlessly prompting all the applicants to keep their distance.

"Wow, cleanup," Jarvis announced excitedly. And then silently to himself, *They must have a very bad team if they want me to be cleanup.*

"So, you want the job?"

"Yea, I'll take it."

We pay cash, kid, the end of the day. You want to start now?"

"Sure, but I'll need to go home and get my glove." *"One of my more ridiculous assertions,"* Jarvis admitted shaking his head

"Glove? We probably have some. Hey Ted," the man called out. "The kid here is going to do some cleanup. Get him a pair of gloves, will ya."

"Sure boss." They winked at each other, and for reasons Jarvis still couldn't fathom, he winked back at them, as if they were all in a special club.

While walking behind the tattooed man, because his arms were a roadmap of designs, he saw a couple of friends and waved. *Won't they be jealous when I tell them I'm being paid to play some baseball!* Jarvis thought proudly. It put a bounce in his step until he and Ted stopped beside four large pens behind the tent.

"Phew, it stinks. Is this where you keep the elephants?"

"Yep, it sure is kid. Here are your gloves, and over there is a shovel. You see those mounds of shit. Have at it. Dump it all in the wheelbarrow, and I'll show you where it goes. His mocking leer only deepened Jarvis's annoyance and humiliation.

"Know where I'd like to put it," he muttered, but already had spent the money he would make.

CHAPTER SIX

Jarvis watched his son pull away from the house in his truck, "A Silverado, I think," he said peering toward the street and waving. *Great truck. Michael deserves it. But the darn thing costs as much as the first house Molly and I bought. His payments are probably more than the one hundred dollars we paid each month.*

They had been sitting in the screened front porch for almost an hour, yakking about a lot of things. It was his seventy-fifth birthday, and neither of his children had forgotten. Shelly had visited the day before with the two boys. *They were like two horses pawing and snorting at the starting gate until she told them to spend ten minutes with me, and then they could play on their I-pads again. Guess I don't provide the same kind of excitement. I know they love me though. Apparently television isn't the babysitter Molly and I occasionally used it for when the kids were younger. Course it was a great time to raise children. They were usually outside playing with friends and using their imagination. Ah, a feat this new generation might find difficult.* Jarvis reached for the lite beer and took a sip. "Blah, not cold anymore," he muttered. It was a warm day with only a wisp of wind, but the fan overhead, and his body's aging thermostat allowed him to be comfortable.

Michael had been their problem child, full of energy, and obstinate, like a pup who objected to peeing outside. *Thank God, Molly's teaching background helped channel his, "energy". She was good that way.* Jarvis cracked a smile when he remembered how their son had dragged out the delivery into the tenth hour, and Molly had yelled through gritted teeth, "This one's going to be a bastard."

She never faulted Michael for punishing her that way and was always more patient with him than his sister. Jarvis was glad his son eventually outgrew the stubbornness and self-absorption which had followed him through middle school, and then like magic, changed along with his voice. Now he was a successful accountant, divorced, but dating, and seemed happy. Jarvis's philosophy, "Happiness cannot be over-rated. It garnishes the need to get out of bed in the morning."

"Michael, I'm so glad you came over."

"Dad, it is your birthday. Seventy-four, right?"

"Good guess, but wrong. Seventy-five, but I like seventy-four better. Your sister was over yesterday. Those boys are growing up fast."

There was an indulgent nod from his son, but the eyes flashed the message, "You've told me that a thousand times."

"And I'll probably say it a thousand more times," Jarvis thought.

"Here Dad," Michael said, passing over an envelope. "I didn't get you a gift. Hope you don't mind."

"What, and break a tradition? No, at my age a card is fine. They're always good for a laugh." He removed the card and held it away from his body until the buffoonish remarks came into focus. "Do you really look this old?" And inside, "or did you sleep on your face all night?" Jarvis feigned an uncontrollable guffaw.

Michael had written, "Don't tell me this is what I'm going to look like when I get older."

"No way," Jarvis replied. "If you're lucky, you'll be half as good looking as I am."

"Ha," Michael resounded. "At least your sense of humor hasn't changed."

"Some things have," Jarvis said, presenting a more serious front to the conversation. He snorted. "Your mother didn't like it when I used the word "things". She wanted specificity. Always the English teacher. Always correcting. You kids too." His son nodded with a smile.

"Anyway, glad you came over. I want to speak with you about something besides my birthday. Read an article the other day, and realized it is time for the talk."

"Ah, little late for that dad." Michael joked.

Jarvis smirked. "Figured you would have a comeback. No, I mean before the final curtain drops."

Michael pulled back and watched his father warily. "What are you saying? You sick?"

"Just what Shelly asked. Nothing to worry about, but I am at the age when things happen. Don't have many friends left. Some moved out of state, others have taken the celestial Uber to Heaven, they hope. A few are too sick or confused to take care of themselves. I want you to be my Power of Attorney. You know, to manage my finances and pay the bills if I'm unable to do it." He stopped and looked at Michael in disbelief. "Can you believe I'm willing to trust you with my money."

"It is shocking."

Shelly will be the Medical Power of Attorney. We both know she's tough as nails and will be able to make the difficult health decisions when I near the last rung on the ladder." Jarvis chuckled. "I won't forget the day she came home, a little annoyed that she had to punch some boy who was teasing her girlfriend. Gave him a blackeye according to the young man's father. The dad was quite angry until I told him why Shelly had swung at his son. I can still hear the man saying, "Your daughter?" Ended the conversation right there." He wiggled a finger at Michael to emphasize his next point. "Amazing how your personalities switched when you entered your teens. Shelly developed this in your face, let's tackle the problem head on attitude. You preferred taking your time and studying all sides of an issue. You also became quite the thespian if I remember correctly."

"Your flattery keeps overwhelming me dad. Guess you don't remember those six months Shelly called me the lesbian in the family."

Jarvis chuckled. "Understandable mistake."

"Really?"

"You survived."

"Yea, I put a toad in her drawer, and it peed all over her clothes. I told her I'd do it again if she didn't stop."

"I kind of liked the originality of that," Jarvis said, with a gleam in his eyes. "Had to punish you though. Your mother thought you needed counseling." Both men grinned. "Your Uncle Ken was five years younger than she was. Must have been a saint for a brother. I don't recall her ever talking about any stunts he may have done." He took a sip from the cold beer on the table, and then leaned back with his hands behind his head.

"Don't want to sound maudlin, but birthdays come too fast anymore. Makes one reflective." Jarvis's attention swept past the confines of the screen porch to the montage of family photos he could hazily see hanging in the hallway to his bedroom. The kids had lifted them from the albums Molly had meticulously put together and presented it as a gift to their parents for Christmas one year. They were about eight and ten at the time. *One of the best gifts ever. Molly didn't seem concerned about where the pictures came from, just loved* the *ingenuity and thoughtfulness.*

Jarvis could feel a prodding on his shoulder. "Hey dad, I'm over here."

"Sorry. Mind wanders sometimes."

"Just want to say that you make me proud."

Jarvis chuckled. "Isn't that my line to you and your sister?"

"I stole it from the best."

"Stealing, huh? Now your mother would say there are two bad eggs in the family." Jarvis leaned forward and grabbed Michael's arm. His eyes prefaced the words that quietly tripped out of his mouth. "Glad you inherited my genes. Gets lonely at the bottom of the pecking order."

That afternoon, after Michael left, he slept longer than usual, tumbling into a well of memories that spilled a hint of loosed revelry across his face.

"I blame the slices of birthday cake I've eaten," Jarvis whispered to himself upon awakening. "All the fat and sugar from yesterday and today made me sleepy. Molly would have been slapping my hands if I reached for another piece." He laid his head back, and linked his fingers across his belly, evidence of contented happiness stretching across his face.

It was their fifth wedding anniversary, "Nineteen eighty-four." It was a period of wistful dreams and unrelenting love. Molly had hyperventilated with surprise when he gave her the Aerosmith tickets. A slight exaggeration, but she did exclaim that it was one of the best gifts she ever got. *Nothing like reinforcing the passion with a little Rock and Roll and Walk this Way.*

In as much as the concert's throbbing chords, and songs unraveled his inhibitions, it was the loudly shared enthusiasm of the audience that pulled Jarvis into its clamorous appeal. For a few hours, he and Molly set aside the sobering reality waiting for them on the other side of the stadium walls. It wasn't frightful, but it could be taxing at times.

It seemed everyone was standing, or dancing, and shouting familiar words as the band played their strident bars of music. Back then, ice chests could be brought in without being checked for alcohol and there was plenty of that. And the distinct smell of pot seemed to come in on a breeze that shrouded at least their whole section of the stadium. Neither he nor Molly had ever been big fans. Admittedly a few tokes at college, "but outside of that, nothing Jarvis was aware of.

"This is great," Jarvis screamed, grinning, and swaying his arms over his head to the beat.

"Woo!" Molly yelled. "Five years baby!" She wrapped her arms around him and planted a sloppy one on his mouth. "Another beer for our anniversary!" she cried, swiping sweaty strings of hair away from her face. "Woo!"

"Happy fifth," Jarvis repeated between swigs from his own can.

"Hey mister." the young man next to him shouted, as he accidently wobbled into them. He wore a t-shirt which read, "Question Everything. The World is Flat." "You and your woman having an anniversary? How about a toke," and thrust the joint in front of Jarvis's face. "It's our gift to you," he said elbowing the giggly blond next to him.

"Yea. Sure," she squealed exuberantly. "An anniversary, huh? Wow!" She waved a hand of encouragement at Jarvis. "What's your name?"

A little glassy eyed, Jarvis observed self-righteously. *Wonder what I look like? But we're having such a great time.* He glanced at Molly clinging to his arm and simpered. *Especially my wife.*

Then focusing back on his spirited neighbors, "Ah, name is Jarvis."

"A "J" for Mr. Jarvis. Isn't that funny." Around them people were starting to chant "Toys in the Attic!" including Molly who was blasting the words in his face.

"Well, I don't know," Jarvis drawled, "Been a long time."

"Go ahead Mr. J for joint," the blond encouraged tittering. "Just once, and then let your wife take a toke. Try to hold it in."

"Oh, what the hell," Jarvis said, inhaling deeply. "it's for the anniversary!"

"Me too!" Molly said, grabbing the blunt, and sucking in. "Whew, that was great," she squealed afterward.

"Looked like a pro," Jarvis teased.

"Love this. Woo!" she screamed, raising her arms and gyrating to the music. "Yea baby!"

"You sexy thing," Jarvis shouted.

Several hours later, they were driving home, captured in the glow of the moon's reflection as it lit the road in front of them. *Glad it's full,* Jarvis thought. *And the coffee helped a little bit. Hmm, not many lights along this stretch.* The excitement of the evening was wearing off and the thumping in his head was beginning to recede. He had turned the radio down low, but now the somnolent urges of the music's lulling whisper, and the fatiguing weight of overzealous partying flirted with his ability to stay awake. He peeked over at Molly, figuring she would be asleep, but instead, wanton eyes, and a devilish smile greeted his curiosity.

"I had a wonderful time. Thank you. Woo," she attempted weakly.

Sounded like a hoarse owl, Jarvis thought amusedly.

She listed over and kissed him on the cheek. As she leaned back, Molly winked at him, and with beguiling suggestiveness, lazily curled her tongue around her lips. "I'm feeling very naughty," she purred. "Very naughty."

"Whoa. Is this my wife?" Jarvis murmured, casting glances in her direction. His eyes widened as she began to unbutton the front of her shirt.

"So hot in here," she whispered huskily.

"Can agree with that," Jarvis, said feeling moisture on his palms beginning to form. Normally Molly would be swallowed up in the darkness, but tonight, the moon's radiance partially brightened her side of the car and highlighted the fullness of her breasts as she pulled open the shirt.

She kept peeking over at him as she shrugged her shoulders, and let the shirt slip off her arms. Then she popped open the front of her bra.

"*Got to keep my eyes straight ahead*," Jarvis reminded himself, but the carnal invitation bribed his resistance. "Molly, what are you doing?" he squeaked.

"I'm being very naughty." She traced her fingers over her bare flesh, circling her nipples, and wetting her lips again."

"Damn Molly!" Jarvis said tightly and tugged on his pants. He had seen her breasts a hundred times, but never in the car when he was driving and still contending with the aftereffects of a concert.

"You like them, don't you?"

"Yes, but I'm going to get in an accident."

She pushed her breasts together. "You like it when I do this," she said in a sultry voice.

"Like? I love it!" Jarvis exclaimed, and then "Oh shit," as the car hit a pothole, and the front tire on the passenger side suddenly caused them to veer to the right. There was a loud clumping sound, until he was able to bring the automobile to a stop.

"Damn," Jarvis muttered. "A flat!"

"I'm so sorry," Molly sputtered nervously, her breasts now covered by the shirt she had thrown across her chest.

"Not your fault," Jarvis muttered, "Well, not entirely your fault," and grinned. "You wanted to give me a thrill. You're just so, I don't know, erotic, I couldn't keep my eyes off you."

"I've never done anything like this before," Molly confessed contritely. She hesitantly giggled.

Jarvis grabbed her elbow and pulled her over for a kiss. "Let me get out and check the tire. I love you so much."

"Still?"

"Very much." He kissed his wife again, this time his tongue playing tag with hers. "If I had a blanket in the back, I'd throw it on the ground, and make love with you right now."

"Probably be rough."

"Very rough," Jarvis said, caressing her cheek.

"How bad is it," Molly asked when he got back into the car.

"Just needs the spare, but even with the moonlight, it's too dark to change safely. Might as well recline the seats and try to get some sleep. Fix it in the morning."

Grunting, Jarvis twisted around to face his naughty passenger, contorting his body so it would comfortably conform to the curve in the seat. "Not too bad," he murmured. He reached out with his hand, and cautiously snaked it under Molly's shirt and bra. "Mind if I cop a feel?"

His wife smiled. "Only if you let me do the same."

Jarvis started to undo a few buttons on his shirt.

"Oh no, mister. Not there." and pulled on the front of his belt.

CHAPTER SEVEN

Despite the absence of any specific chores to do, Jarvis expected the morning to be like most of the others. It would stampede through the hours until it was time for lunch, and then the afternoon hobble along because of the infestation of boredom. He had to admit that when Molly died, she seemed to have siphoned off some of the verve, and enthusiasm that together was a hallmark of their life.

However, today, even the morning hours seemed to lope along, maybe because the drapes hadn't been pulled tight, and sunlight ambushed him an hour before he usually got up. "Wonder what idiot didn't close them all the way?" he growled, smacking the side of his head. "Me! The kids say I need my beauty sleep, or I can be a bit ornery." He harrumphed. "I don't believe that. I can be ornery any time, sleep or no sleep. And I'm way past needing the beauty part."

Waking up early ruined the promise to sleep in on the weekends, like Shelly suggested. "Relish moments to just do nothing. You earned it pops."

A shadow of transient contention blighted his demeanor. *Doesn't know what she's talking about. Never been able to just lay in bed like Molly. The legs are over the side as soon as my eyes open. To be awake, and just stare at the ceiling. Not in my nature. Got to be doing something.*

Although afternoons ticked along slowly, he recently told his daughter, "It seems perverse that the weeks, and months appear to slip away so much faster." *As if there is a sudden rush for me to reach the end of the line,* he concluded reluctantly to himself. "Can the year really be going by so quickly? I look forward to those moments when you yell at the boys, although not as often as I recall your mother, and I needed to yell at you and your brother."

"Oh dad, you're such a comedian," she teased.

"What? You think I was kidding about Military School?"

"Of course, you weren't," she said playing along. "As much as mom threatening to shove your running shorts and sweaty T-shirt into somebody's pillowcase, who shall be nameless, because he kept dropping them on the floor."

Jarvis flashed a flippant smile. "Ah, she was quite serious about that. Now, if I may continue, I want to live long enough to witness Democrats and Republicans inviting each other over for backyard picnics." Shelley looked askance at him on that one. "And finally, to visit parts of the country I've only seen on the Travel Channel."

"A short, but heartfelt list, I'm sure," Shelly said. "Well, you've heard me do my share of shouting dad, so you can cross that one off your bucket list, or whatever list that is."

"Suppose I can," and they both cackled at their private joke.

"And maybe you can accompany the family on our trip to Yellowstone. We have the RV. But the bipartisan backyard picnic to roast marshmallows? More likely to see them skewering each other or pushing someone into the fire."

"Good way to put it," Jarvis said with a sniggering grin.

"Oh, and about time going faster," she opined boastfully. "I read it's because we have so many new experiences when we're younger and then as we get older, things become habitual and expected."

"Except for our bodies wearing away and parts breaking down." Jarvis interjected.

"Of course," Shelly said nodding compliantly. "And by the time people retire, they've already had a lot of years under their belt. Just like you dad. A lot of years under your belt."

"You're getting as sarcastic as Michael," Jarvis bantered. "Good seeing you come out of your shell. You're what, forty?"

Shelly challenged the remark with a sassy smile.

Jarvis reciprocated with one of his own, and then gazed proudly at her. "So smart, and always the teacher, just like your mother."

"No, it's just because we're women," she said jauntily.

Jarvis grumpily kicked his way out of bed and vowed sticking to the routine. Thirty minutes later the old guy plopped into his favorite living room chair. When he turned on the TV, his eyes widened gleefully. His traffic girl rarely worked weekends, yet there she was, sitting in for one of the news anchors. "Don't like the way you cut your hair," he said to her. "Too short. Next time get my opinion. My wife did. Course then she usually did what she wanted anyway."

He scratched the wisps of gray hair on the side of his head and smirked. He was reminded of the brief stint of rebelliousness the summer after he graduated college and would be entering Navy flight school in the fall. *Always had my hair short for the ROTC program during* school *and decided to grow it a little longer, just to try it out. The Navy put a quick stop to that.*

Jarvis never thought participating in NROTC was extraordinary because his father and his father before him had each served at least four years for their country. It seemed only natural and, "Well, patriotic," he told his grandsons in his most conciliatory manner. They were ten and twelve at the time. He supposed they had become somewhat jaded to his pedantic intrusions, but it wasn't like he accosted them every day. "The allegiance to country seems to be missing from recent generations."

He didn't do it to chastise them, or even drop a hint, but to let a part of his history become an engraved part of theirs'. "My father used to tell us how blessed he was to live in America. And with that privilege came responsibility to continue the sojourn of his father to protect the rights and liberties the country has fought so gallantly for over two centuries. When I was your age, most parades in town, particularly ones having some military significance, would have a small contingent of veterans marching, and possibly even a tank. And when the flag passed, everyone stood up, and placed their hand over their heart. It was sacrilege if you didn't."

As Jarvis reflected upon it, a despondent expression briefly rolled across his face. *"Yea times sure are different."*

The boys had been respectful enough, with no eye-rolling, or bored glances, and Jarvis hoped it was because they recognized the importance of what he was saying. He didn't want them to be nice just because he was Pops or their mother had threatened them with having to read a real book, and not something online.

It was nineteen sixty-five, the Vietnam war was becoming a nightly obsession on television and competed with the racial strife Americans contended with on the home turf. There was no girlfriend on the horizon except in vivid dreams. He had just graduated college with NROTC experience in his back pocket, and raucous, long-haired guys from across the Atlantic were searing the states with their own kind of musical commentary. It should have been no surprise to his family when he had applied for navy flight training. Except that it was, and unpredictably, his dad was the one debating the decision.

"That's just insane. Risking your life for what, to prevent a Communist incursion into southeast Asia? It's already happened." Jarvis could still hear the intervening, cynical laugh. "We're fighting this war for whom, the South Vietnamese or our own veneration.

If you want to do four years, or even a career, that's great, and couldn't make me prouder. But to pursue flight training and a probable transfer to an aircraft carrier in that ghastly place, is just crazy. Do you know what the casualty rates are for pilots?"

Jarvis remembered stepping back, dismayed by the old man's opposition, and gauging what to say next. "Dad, I want to fly an F4 Phantom off the deck of an aircraft carrier! If that means I am doing it during some God forsaken war, so be it!"

He would never forget the complexion of frustration and anger staring back at him. "He just turned around and left," he told Molly a couple days after his father's funeral. "Didn't speak to me for a year. It wasn't until I had gotten out, my mother informed me that dad claimed to have this premonition I would be killed in a conflict he completely disagreed with, and the fact I had not chosen the branch of the military he had served in. Semper fidelis How strange is all that?"

Jarvis pushed down on the arms of the recliner, and briefly lifted himself up to relieve the pressure pushing up into his rectum. Molly used to tease that he had a boney ass, although not using exactly those words. "I need more of a cushion back there, huh?" he would joke. After nestling down into the leather again, and closing his eyes, splotches of memories from his training days in Pensacola and his subsequent deliverance into the war seeped into his rumination.

Flight school had been every bit as demanding as the rumors purported it would be. Jarvis guessed God must have been looking over his shoulder because he had this innate sense about him whenever he got into the cockpit, and even the technical, and sometimes tedious blackboard instruction came naturally to him. His body and mind not only tolerated the rigor of the constant drilling, but relished the competitive demands that came with it. The old man had been right, however. Twenty-four hours after getting his wings, Jarvis was deployed to a carrier in the Gulf of Tonkin.

Most of the experiences on and off ship were embedded in corners of his brain reserved for brief, and solemn visits that only fellow aviators would understand. But periodically, Jarvis jotted down a few, hoping Michael and Shelly might read them after he was gone. Unfortunately, most of his flying buddies had already departed on their last sortie into the wild blue, and were permanently buzzing the clouds, high, overhead. Despite all the years which had passed, there was one incident which behaved like a kamikaze whenever it appeared on the horizon of his recollections. It pounded away at his soul and never failed to bring a wet haze over his eyes.

He was three quarters of a mile out, and closing fast on his moving target, a five-hundred-foot runway, atop a one hundred-thousand-ton aircraft carrier. The sea was angry, and the ship pitched and yawed, making the landing trickier than usual. *Definitely a controlled crash today,* Jarvis thought with obdurate determination.

"Coming in a little low Big Turkey," the voice over the radio announced.

"Roger that," Jarvis responded, increasing the thrust, and lifting the head of the Phantom. It had been a successful flight, if one considered dropping Napalm on innocent women and children something to be proud of. "It really sucks," he had said to one of his trusted new brothers. "It's a mission. I get it. And orders are orders. But I sure wish the damn Viet Cong would have the balls to march through a field, instead of hiding themselves in the jungle or those damn little villages."

After thirty-four bombing missions into the North, he could usually bury that remorse deep within him, and be thrilled like a kid racing a four-wheeler through the woods. The differences of course being that the Phantom weighed forty-four thousand pounds, cost three and a half million dollars, and was approaching its present destination at one hundred and fifty miles per hour. Ten minutes before it had been traveling 1,300 miles per hour.

The plan was for Jarvis to hit the lighted "ball" on the control panel straight on and snag any one of the four arresting cables with the tailhook underneath the Phantom II. Working with an ideal distance of two hundred feet, it would yank the jet to a jerking halt, and prevent it from going over the side. Simultaneously Jarvis had to be sure he had enough "touch and go" speed, just in case he failed to hook one of the cables and had to take off again. "Awesome motivation not to fail," he had told one of the new pilots.

"Tailhook down. Landing gear down," Jarvis said rattling off the sequence out loud. "Flaps down a notch."

"Looking good," the Landing Signal officer announced.

"Gotta please God," Big Turkey thought. "Flaps down full now. In the groove, and intercepting glide path," he reported to the LSO. In front of Jarvis, the orange orb on the screen bounced ever so slightly above the horizontal green display of lights. That was the ship heaving up and down on the choppy ocean. "Keep it level," he kept reminding himself over and over. The ship was down in a trough but coming up quickly. "Leveling out. Now! Yes! Got you," Jarvis yelled as he trapped the number three arresting wire with the tailhook and tensed slightly for the abrupt wrench backward. Except it never came.

"Oh shit! The cable snapped!" he shouted, instinctively reaching for the ejection lever as the jet hurtled over the edge of the ship.

Abruptly Jarvis could feel his body crushed against the seat, and his skull hammered against the headrest as he exploded into the air. Moments later, his breath returned as he began to float down under the canopy of the chute. For an instant he could still see sailors diving and jumping to avoid the cable which maddeningly whipped across the deck like a pissed off snake. Then he had to focus on saving his own life in the heaving sea.

Later, he found out two men had been killed, and five injured. It was equipment failure, and not his fault, but he couldn't pack those senseless deaths away. They persecuted him on and off for three years with sporadic bouts of tremors and sweats. But time, counseling, and prayerful intervention, finally exonerated his feelings of guilt, and responsibility. In war, men will die.

However, more than the psychological trauma, it was the neck injury that ended his career as an aviator. Surgeons had to remove two lamellae in his cervical spine that were giving him pain, and weakness in his arms, and then fuse several vertebrae together. Unfortunately, this prevented him from looking completely right or left, and that was never good for someone who wanted to fly.

After all these years, Jarvis still wasn't sure what persuaded him to try Real Estate, but it turned out to be a career decision that satisfactorily filled the void an honorable discharge from the Navy left behind. He was offered the opportunity to teach jet avionics, but the thought of being stuck in front of a blackboard while others were flying would be like shoving a shiv into his gut. The sight and sound of screaming jets taunting him every day.

CHAPTER EIGHT

Jarvis was waxing his "baby", a platinum, 2010 Infinity G37, "My James Bond car", he would josh with friends. "Can't afford an Aston Martin." Once a month he would spend time maintaining its luster, and every six months it would get an oil and filter change. "Three point seven liters with three hundred and thirty-three horses. A real stallion when it takes off," he'd recite proudly to anyone who wanted to listen.

But ever since Shelly had taken his keys away, the car had not moved from its spot for five weeks. Well, that's what Jarvis wanted her to believe.

"Dad, you've gotten two tickets in the past three weeks, and you don't drive that often. The last one because you went through a stop."

"So, I accidently forgot to brake. I didn't do it on purpose. Let me keep the keys, and I promise to be more careful."

"No."

"Well, what if I promise not to drive again." He surveyed her countenance for any compliant acceptance, but she pulled back and eyed him with an "Oh, really," disbelief.

"What?" he asked innocently.

"You never did have a good poker face, dad. I'm not that gullible. The temptation would be too great. I want you, and everybody else on the road to be safe."

"Don't have to reprimand me," he had returned, a bit harsher than planned.

"Dad..."

"Alright! Give me a second!" He dug into his pants pocket and fished around. "Here they are," he muttered, dropping the keys into Shelly's palm.

When she turned to put them in her purse, he surreptitiously whispered, "Wondered when this might happen. That's why I have two more sets."

"Now, where is the spare key, Dad?" Shelly asked knowingly. "You always had one for emergencies."

"Uh, that's what I needed to do the other day," Jarvis said smacking his head.

"Dad! The other key. And don't be grumpy."

"Alright, I'll get it," he groused, scuffing into the kitchen. *She thinks she's so smart.* He grabbed the key from the hook by the back door and lollygagged back into the living room. His daughter's hand was out in front of her.

"Alright! Alright!" Jarvis growled. "Now you have my keys. Happy!" He glared at Shelly, hoping to see some guilty remorse surface on her face. "Best acting I've ever done," he thought, congratulating himself.

Now in the cool of the morning, he intended to give the Infinity the coat it deserved, and when he was done buffing, he'd sit behind the wheel for a few minutes. Too many vigilant eyes to observe him on the weekend. However, during the week, discretion allowed him to bend the no driving rule when he stealthily went out shopping or drove to the meals site for his volunteering.

"Hey Jarvis, looks good," Steve Parker shouted from the sidewalk, inviting himself up the macadam to admire the car. He was a male nurse, among the most incongruous terms Jarvis had ever heard. Right up there with the oncologist saying, "your father has non-small cell lung cancer, lower mortality than small cell," "Ah, cancer is cancer when it comes to family. None of this statistical degree stuff, a retort Jarvis had bridled because the impulsive anger was born out of resentment towards his father's years of smoking.

His neighbor was a lanky guy, reminding him of Abe Lincoln. He had deep set, blue gray eyes, hazel is what Molly would have called them, and a reassuring gaze which could help calm a man who had just lost his wife. Steve lived two doors down with his wife Cheryl, and their two boys. Jarvis suspected that one of his own kids, probably Shelly, the mother hen, had asked the Parkers to keep an eye on dear old dad. *Thinks he's fifty and can still do everything himself. Such nonsense,* Jarvis thought. *I think I'm forty.*

Steve did a lot of walking which was easy to figure out why when

Jarvis met his wife. *Is this woman ever going to shut up. She should have been an auctioneer.*

"Any new aches or pains?" Steve asked, pulling from the usual repertoire of questions.

"No, just the same ones. Helps to keep busy. You?"

"None at the moment, but when I get to be your age."

Jarvis grunted his amusement. "You're a funny guy Steve but stick to your day job. Believe me, getting old is like being rolled. You just don't expect it."

The other man flicked his head back in puzzlement. "Rolled? What does that mean?"

"Showing your age neighbor or maybe what part of the country you grew up in. Means getting mugged." Jarvis grinned. *Guess I stumped him, he* thought with a shade of arrogance. "Say, just curious, but how did you and Cheryl meet? Molly would have been the one to know stuff like that."

"At the hospital. I was taking care of her father. Gave her my number and said to call me if she had any questions." He smiled. "Don't know how ethical that was, but the next day she called, and told me there was one question. Would I be free Friday night for dinner?" Steve shrugged nonchalantly. "Guess I was. How about you?"

"Oh, we bumped into each other, literally. Her car into mine. Not much damage. Told her I wouldn't tell the Insurance company if she went out with me."

"Bribery, huh."

"Would have been forty-one years last month."

"Wow. What's the secret?"

"Selling your soul to the devil."

"Ha-ha."

"Actually, just keeping her happy as possible."

"Oh." The younger man momentarily mulled the answer before continuing, "Had an interesting conversation with the twelve year old the other day. He told me about this new video app called WW II. Wanted to find out if I knew what the WW stood for." He peered down at the hood and gritted his teeth."

"Pass the reflection test?" Jarvis asked facetiously.

"Huh, yea. I told him his great grandfather fought in World War II." Steve turned his head and looked strangely at Jarvis. "He asked me, "You mean there really was a World War II? Damn. Have I become that old?"

Jarvis laughed empathetically. "My grandsons surprise me the same way every time they visit. Really Steve, the war was almost eighty years ago, immediately after they did away with the chariot and javelin. Its ancient history." He shuffled over to a bench several feet away and sat down. "My problem is the opposite. Now a days, I forget stuff as quickly as I try to learn it. Imagine what it's like for me to struggle with the new technology." He held up his cell. This smart phone is about as techy as I get."

His neighbor laughed. "Reminds me about what happened at the hospital a few months back. The screens began to shut down all over the hospital. Major headache. Ten O'clock at night and Information Systems is trying to fix the problem from home. Despite my lack of expertise, I suggested that maybe the room where the mainframe is kept might be too hot. I had heard the hardware needs to be in a cool environment. Nah, couldn't be that. I go home, and the next day find out IS finally came in at three in the morning. Guess what the problem was... a thermostat in the room had broken, or whatever. Me, the genius."

Jarvis smirked. *What a world. The more advanced we become, the dumber we get.* He wiped away the sweat on his forehead, then lifted his arms and took a whiff. "Whew, more deodorant."

"Steve grinned. "Yea, humid today. Well, guess I'll be seeing you Jarvis." He started backing down the drive. "You need anything, don't hesitate to call."

"You're in my contacts," Jarvis replied, holding up the cell again. "He's a good man," he murmured, watching Steve disappear down the street.

After a drink of water, a banana, and cookie, Jarvis sat down in the living room, and relished the coolness of the fan blowing on him. But it couldn't dissipate the stubborn annoyance reflected on his face. "How I can be sapped of energy so quickly," he griped. "I was outside only an hour and a half." He sighed resignedly. "Just having a bad day." He closed his eyes, and with half-hearted reluctance, finally gave in to the somnolent overtures of his body.

It was the first Christmas without Molly. The holiday was her favorite time of the year and brought her joy to bring down all the seasonal boxes and decorate. Yuletide music, and gingerbread fragrances would fill the air. The tree was always a family project, and even after the kids moved out, the family would get together to put on the lights, colorful balls, and other ornamental trinkets. It was so festive and uplifting that even Jarvis felt invigorated by the spirit of it all.

He and Molly used to visit the city, and bask in all the Yule time bliss, the twinkling trees, the screamingly happy children, and the tipsy laughter of spirited adults. They would stroll hand in hand, sharing whispered tidbits of reminisces, and spice it with giggles. Occasionally they would stop in front of a store window and stand like wide eyed children at the animated displays, then point and nudge each other when one of them saw something new down the street.

Jarvis was back in the city, alone, more to silence the kids' preaching that he go out, and do something for the holiday, then encouraging himself to discover some of the old excitement. But today, as he trudged down the city sidewalk, snowy drips of sadness continued to splash away the joy and happiness that used to warm his heart. Without Molly at his side, the trip was more of an ordeal than a revival of his soul. Faces stared back at him, blank or impatient, and harsh pleas demanded him to, "Walk faster old man." Children screamed they were hungry, and parents warned them that Santa wouldn't come if they didn't behave.

Jarvis brushed away some of the white flakes covering a bench, and plopped down on its cold, wet surface. In his coat pocket he clutched the large golden key Molly had given him one Christmas many years ago. One of those that might open imaginary castle doors, or fanciful gates to enchanted gardens. Inscribed on it were the words, "You unlocked my love."

It was the best gift she ever gave him.

Now when he rolled it around in his fingers, it provided him with strength, and a montage of memories that pushed away the tears lingering in his eyes. He could hear Molly's voice asking him one December where they should put the nativity. "Let's be different this year, Jarvis. Make it a simple Christmas, symbolic of the Christ child's birth."

Then she glided around the room, like a sprite flicking her wand, seemingly making the balsam suddenly appear on the mantle, and curl around the railings on the stairs. "Do you feel its wafting scent tickle the inside of your nose," she asked him.

"I think I do. I think I do," he said to her with a smile. "Wafting. Molly used words like that. She was an English teacher, and reveled in them like a child playing in a pile of leaves.

"Words can give life," he remembered her telling Michael and Shelly. "Hurtful ones can sting for a very long time."

Suddenly Jarvis didn't feel so bad. He could see and hear clearly now. Strangers were dancing past him carrying brightly colored packages of all shapes and sizes. They shouted Merry Christmas to everyone they saw including Jarvis. Some of them even nodded knowingly at him, as if they knew that his smothering grief had given way to a revived holiday spirit.

A little girl wearing a red coat, with a furry white collar came up to him, and said, "Don't be sad Mister. Mommy says Jesus loves you. Here, you can have my candy cane," and then pranced away from him with a selfless giggle.

Jarvis's smile was so big it was practically a grin. He looked at the empty spot next to him on the bench. "You're sitting right there, aren't you baby?" he said.

CHAPTER NINE

Jarvis had been out food shopping, and now he was home, recuperating. His trips were purposely brief, and cannily done after the closest neighbors had gone to work. After he parked the car, he would walk nonchalantly up to the store, yet always keeping an eye out for familiar faces. Once inside, he repeated the same process with each, and every aisle. He didn't know who the kids may have told about taking away his driving privileges, and he didn't want to get caught. "If they find out I still had another copy of the key, the Infinity might be next!"

There was never much to buy, because he usually gave Shelly a doctored list, and she bought the items with his credit card. Something he welcomed, because shopping was one of his least favorite things to do. Although now it presented an opportunity for him to get out and drive. His modus operandi had always been simple. When going to a store, know what you want, buy it, and leave. It was like he was wearing blinders, and nothing would distract him. Molly said it was a guy thing and took the enjoyment out of the whole experience. "Shopping is an experience?" he asked her on more than one occasion.

Normally he wouldn't be tired after one of his *excursions*, but Jarvis had been caught up in what he called a limbo sleep the night before. One of those deceptively drowsy states, where he may have been asleep, but oddly, could hear all the discordant sounds around him. He didn't try opening his eyes because that might validate the fear that he actually was awake, and better to gamely think otherwise.

And then at the store, each aisle had been like an obstacle course, with people staggered from one end to the other just to test his patience. "Ah, to be so popular," Jarvis moaned. "But what a pain in the ass." Even the self check-out had five people waiting in line to thwart his expeditious departure.

He took a sip of his rum and coke, more soda than alcohol since he was older now. "Ghrarrr, crowds aggravate me!" He pushed hard against the back of the recliner, so the leg part would kick up. "Don't do this very often," he mumbled admiring the drink, "not at eleven thirty in the morning. But all those people tested my sanity." He reached for his cell, tapping on the screen twice, and then begrudgingly, perused the trail of emails he had gotten. "Such crap," he remarked out loud. "My generation got along fine without e-mails and texts, and Instagram, whatever the hell that is."

Jarvis closed his eyes, and the phone fell to the floor. *My poor Molly. Didn't she get sucked in* was the last thought he had before succumbing to the tendrils of imposing sleep.

He jerked awake, his butt numb, his pants wedged into his crack, and his vision blinded by the sun. Then he realized it was just the hot glow from the floor lamp next to the lounge chair.

"Fell asleep," he grumbled. "Wonder what time it is?" and looked at the clock on the mantle. "Only forty minutes?" His skin felt moist, and there was pounding in his chest, like drums in an old Western movie. For a few seconds, he expected Molly to walk into the room, much as she did in one of the scenes which had intruded upon his sleep, and then realized she had died two years before. Remnants of the dreams dug out silent memories which Jarvis had carefully packed away, and now were beginning to surface.

She was a good woman, and a good wife and mother, Jarvis thought affirmatively. *That can never be taken away from her.* Furrows of frustration lined his brow. *What's been done, is done, and I will never be able to make it right. Hmm, haven't looked at the Journal in a while. Though why should I? Must be a glutton for punishment.*

He pushed up out of the chair, groaning at the grating pain in his stiff hips, and hobbled over to the old, wooden chest where he kept his most secret possessions. He had kept it out in the old shed when Molly was alive, away from an accidental discovery. In it were the old letters and jotted thoughts which littered different parts of his life. He dug underneath them and pulled out the blue notebook.

"It's been a long time," Jarvis acknowledged, touched by the power it wielded just being held in his hands. He still questioned why he had written about his infidelity. Well, he was sure that's what Molly would have called it, and over time, so did he.

Perhaps, Jarvis opined, *this is meant to be an admission of guilt. Some kind of catharsis. Every time I read these pages, I feel chastened. For some reason, the Lord saw fit to rescue me before I completely tattered my integrity and was contemptibly unfaithful to the woman I truly loved.*

Because of observations he had made, and stories he had heard from other couples, Jarvis had come to believe marriages were naturally bipolar, sometimes manic, and sometimes just plain depressing. The trick was to find the balance between the two, and not get stuck in a repetitive loop of discord and remorse. He had witnessed spouses who were unable to blend their distinctive personalities, or tolerate each other's idiosyncrasies, because compromise had become an anathema. Then the walls of the relationship were bound to crack, and ultimately wound the security of their tethered love.

In an instant, Jarvis could replay the scenario that thrashed the fragility of the vows he and Molly had taken the day they got married. Those weeks were a mixture of heady exuberance, chiding guilt, and until the end, presumptive innocence.

He remembered them so well, it was as if the flirtatious betrayal had ended only days before. A perennial reminder that leading with the head and not the teasing lust of the heart and loins strengthened the importance of a good marriage.

He met Joanna at a 5K. A race that was 3.1 miles long through the streets of downtown Boonton. But it could have been any town. The morning had been warm and dry, wrung free of humidity by the previous night's rain. A perfect day for running. There were about two hundred people there, including the restive athletes, and spectators, waiting to shout encouragement to the runners despite heavy breaths and cramping sinews.

It seemed cliché, but he was standing in line, when their eyes first met across the crowded street. Fanciful speculation momentarily ignored Jarvis's promised faithfulness to his wife. He nodded at the woman as if in recognition, and she offered a reciprocating gesture of her own before looking away.

"I'm married anyway," Jarvis scoffed reprovingly. "What is this? Some kind of grandiose, midlife delusion? I'm fifty-two years old." He wished Molly was there to cheer him on, but she had a disdain for hot, smelly bodies lathered in sweat. "Except when mine is hot and sweaty too," she once said with a knowing blink of an eye. But he loved running and the endorphin kick it provided. Besides, an hour ago they did have one of their rare, bruising arguments, debating whether she spent too much money getting her hair and nails done. Foolishness on his part because it was one of the few things Molly did to pamper herself. The 5K was a good distraction. Flirting with another woman certainly wasn't. He turned to the lady behind the table and mentioned his name.

"Medium shirt," he said, thinking he would give it to his wife as a *will you excuse my stupidity* gift. Maybe she'd wear it, maybe she wouldn't, that didn't matter. It was the idea. And if she happened to be in one of those wanton moods of forgiveness, she would strip down in the bedroom, and come back just wearing the shirt. That was a better reward than some blue ribbon.

"Here you go Mr. Heath. Just pin this number to your shorts. Good luck."

"Thanks. Great day for a run. You stay cool."

"Thank you. I'll try," the woman said smiling.

Jarvis had five t shirts from other events he had participated in, *"I really don't need anymore. Glad I decided to give this one to Molly,"* he thought stepping past the table. He tried folding the shirt neatly, but he never was good with corners and sleeves.

"I'll have a medium size," a voice behind him said.

An enticingly, sweet sound, like the drift of music on a hot summer's eve. Jarvis took one more step and attempted to glance inconspicuously over his shoulder. *It's that woman.*

"I'm sorry miss, but another person got the last medium. I have three small, and several large left."

"Oh," the female disappointedly replied. "This is my first race, and I wanted it as a memento to wear."

Hmm, I don't need to give the shirt to Molly, Jarvis argued with the rebuttal in his head. He turned around. "Did I overhear you wanted a medium shirt?"

Intriguing blue eyes stared back at him and invited more of his attention. "I did. Do you have one?"

"I do," he said, and grinned. "Trade you this medium for your large."

"Thank you. I'm not a small, or really big," she stammered. A blush of embarrassment crept upon her face and neck.

Actually, they look quite good to me, Jarvis thought, but rather wisely said, "You look great. I'm sure the man in your life thinks so too."

"Oh, you noticed my diamond," the woman said, sticking up her ring finger. "Actually, I'm divorced. I wear this hoping to keep the men away. The ones I've been meeting are so conceited and rude. Guess I need to be more discriminating." She feigned a guilty smile, and then shrugged her shoulders as a wisp of pensive reflection crossed her face. "It hasn't been easy. I'm always looking for something to distract me. I like to run once in a while, so I figured, why not."

Guess she set me straight, Jarvis thought bemusedly, although his expression must have betrayed whimsical disappointment.

"Oh, sorry," she said sheepishly. "I didn't mean you've been rude. I'm being such a goof today."

Jarvis was amused by the way she rolled her eyes and suffered such humiliation. *Kind of cute.*

"You're married," the woman said pointing to his wedding band.

"Ah, yea, but my wife isn't a fan of these races, and we had an argument this morning. You're not the only one who needs a distraction."

The woman giggled like a schoolgirl, although he guessed she was between thirty-five and forty. He had never been good at guessing a woman's age or weight, something no smart man would even attempt. She had a few sun freckles on her cheeks, and the most beguiling crinkles around her eyes. "I don't even know your name," she remarked holding out her hand.

"Jarvis."

"Jarvis?"

"Yea. It's a long story." *Makes me cringe.*

"Well Jarvis, nice to meet you. I'm Joanna. Thanks again for the shirt."

"My good deed for the day," he teased. "Maybe I'll watch you cross the finish line." And he winked at her. Jarvis rested his next thoughts on the lone cloud above him, and watched it float away. "God, I better get in the car quick when I finish," he warned himself."

He started out fast, maybe subconsciously wanting to impress Joanna, but by the one mile marker, huffing and puffing, and grimacing at his stupidity, Jarvis dropped his pace to a more normal stride. About fifteen seconds later she caught up with him, and winking, mouthed, "I'll see you at the finish line."

"Yikes, she can run. Is this really her first race?" he gasped, and then marveled at the distance she had already put between them.

Despite his grunting breaths, and lagging energy, the Neanderthal in Jarvis briefly stirred thoughts of testosterone fueled imagination. "Cute butt. Looks like she's melted into those shorts. Hmm."

He actually didn't expect to see her again. She needed some distraction, like he did, and happened to get caught up in some idle conversation. But surprisingly, she was waiting for him at the finish line, sucking down a water, and eating a banana.

"You looked real good out there," Joanna said after flagging him down.

"You didn't look so bad yourself," Jarvis returned.

"My running or my butt?" Her eyes glinted mischievously.

"Ha. Ha. Your running of course." He walked over to the closest table and collected a water. "Feels good talking with her," he mused, "but I better make it quick, just like I proposed. Say good-bye, and we go our separate ways." However, when Jarvis twisted around, the lure of her tilted head, and mysterious smile crumbled his defenses.

"Jarvis."

"Huh?"

"I was wondering if it would be too forward of me to ask a married man to celebrate a lady's second place finish?" She beckoned him with a hopeful gaze. "Brunch maybe?"

Brunch? I don't think so, a phantom voice admonished Jarvis. "Uh, second place? Not bad. I didn't know they already announced the results."

"There were only five women running and I followed the first one in."

"Don't you want your ribbon?"

"I told them I had to meet someone, and here you are, and it is," she said waving the award in front of him. "Soo   ?"

"Well, I guess it would be ok," Jarvis drawled cautiously. "Wow, second place."

He didn't expect lunch. A brunch seemed less threatening. *Seems more like a date*, Jarvis reminded himself multiple times following Joanna's decision when and where to meet. *Doesn't feel right*. The nagging reproach lingered, especially after he told Molly he was showing houses to some clients and would be gone for a while. Then when he was taken to a booth in a corner of the restaurant, he really began to doubt the soundness of what he was doing. *This seems too private, but it's only one time*, he assured himself.

Jarvis figured fast food would have been sufficient, and invoke less guilt, but Joanna wanted someplace that served alcohol, and it was her celebration after all. "I don't stink, do I?" she had asked as they were walking back to their cars. "I suddenly remember some things I need to pick up at the store, and then I want to shower." She dipped her left shoulder toward him, and he had foolishly stepped closer to take a sniff. She had been pulling her shirt in and out to cool off, and he accidentally saw her breasts and bra.

Actually, no big deal, Jarvis thought stepping away. *A bra is nothing more than a bikini, right? And how many of those have I seen through the years? Hundreds. It's just that, I've got this ring on my finger, and the sight, well, feels awkward.* He cleared his throat. "Uh, you don't smell sweaty if that's what you mean?" he replied, responding to Joanna's expectant stare.

"Good. See you in an hour."

So here he was, waiting inside Tabor's, just as Joanna had suggested he do if she were a tiny bit late. *Only five minutes so far,* he thought disquietly. *This is wrong. I shouldn't be here. But I feel obligated, and I don't want to disappoint her. Good enough reasons to stay a little bit longer.*

The second hand on the wall clock clicked mercilessly forward. *Maybe she won't show,* he practically pleaded. *Another few minutes, and I'll leave.*

"Jarvis. Hi," Joanna said over his shoulder, and with a gust of enthusiasm. "Glad you came. Didn't know if you'd change your mind." She flounced into the seat on the other side of the table like some teenager on a first date.

"No, I'm here," Jarvis said, forcing an anxious smile. Her arrival made his heartbeat faster, or was it slower? His usual jocular charm seemed to have rolled over and played dead. She was wearing a white t-shirt which said, "I Can Do This", and a dark blue skirt that showed way too much skin for just a celebratory meal. Looking at her, Jarvis figured she would look terrific in anything she chose to wear, or not. *God, this woman is making me crazy,* he noted, with culpable regard. *Calm down. Don't let your imagination get the better of you.*

Jarvis nodded expectantly at the waitress who had come over. "Afternoon folks. A drink mam?"

"A Riesling if you have it."

"Ok. And you sir?"

"The same."

"Be back in a few."

"So, here we are," Joanna said, excitedly a few seconds later. She looked with anticipation at Jarvis.

Guess I'm supposed to say something, he thought, having one of those rare instances when even drivel dried up like a riverbed. Suddenly random inspiration rescued him. "What does the phrase on your shirt mean?"

"I can do this? Being on my own at forty-four." Her eyes strayed beyond Jarvis, and then settled back down. Her demeanor had quickly dissolved from one of adolescent like enthusiasm to one of serious rumination. "Who'd have figured!" she said sharply. "I was able to give him everything, but children. Did he think he was the only one disappointed? But I was thrilled about adopting, even with all the hoops we would have to jump through. He didn't want that." She paused, wrinkling her forehead in consternation. "So, he waited until he found someone else to tell me he no longer loved me and wanted a divorce. Damn him."

"Sorry to hear that. How long have you been divorced?"

"Four months," she said resentfully. "And in this state, the law gave us six months before the divorce was final, in case we changed our minds." She briefly dropped her mouth open and splayed out her hands in front of her as if to say, "Duh, that wasn't going to happen."

The wine arrived, and they gave their meal orders to the waitress.

"Can we toast your second place finish?" Jarvis asked cautiously.

"That would be wonderful. We are supposed to be celebrating that, aren't we."

"Yes, and your first race. I foolishly believed it would be me greeting you at the finish line."

"You were wrong mister smarty pants. But I had all this pent-up anger energizing me." Joanna smiled tentatively. "Forgive me for my outburst before. About the divorce thing."

"Sure," Jarvis said sliding a half grin onto his face. "Forgiven."

"Tell me about you, and your wife. Any children?"

"Plenty to tell there," he warned facetiously. "You have all afternoon?"

Joanna smiled cryptically.

CHAPTER TEN

"I should have seen the danger signs," Jarvis muttered, relapsing into a chastising lament that punished him for disregarding his wife's trust. It was late afternoon and he was sitting in his favorite chair in the living room, shrinking under the bombardment of errant reproach.

Actually, you did, and intentionally ignored them, a quiet brogue advised. Jarvis frowned, and then glanced at the photo of Molly hanging on the wall, the whispered accusation humbling him with its bluntness. It was the last picture of her before she got sick. "What a great smile," he murmured.

He leaned forward, resting his elbows on the tray table, and steepling his hands together in remorseful reflection. It would have been 41 years and instead of observing the abundance of good, "no great times" he and Molly had together, he was roiled in the guilt that came with the deception and knowing impropriety.

He was fifty-two when he fell into the delusion that it was alright to rendezvous with a woman once a week just because she was lonely. Until the very end of the relationship, he gave himself permission to continue the intransigence, by extolling the virtue he was helping her work through this difficult part of her life. *And, until that last* time, *meeting in a restaurant. What an idiot he had been to think it would be safer, and less innocuous?*

He pushed the table to the side and lurched forward, the impetus allowing him to rise and shuffle over to an antique sideboard, where he pulled an old photo album off one of its shelves. "This is the one," he mumbled retracing his steps and sitting back down. He balanced it on his lap, gently turning the pages, and fingering faded images of the family.

"Big, tough guy, aren't I?" he bemoaned. "You never did find out Molly. It would have broken your heart. Joanna was recently divorced and happened to be running a race with me. She came in second for the women and wanted to celebrate her placing. She didn't have anyone with her, and I didn't think it would hurt to meet just once." He steadied the binder on his knees and rubbed his face with the palms of his hands as if that would wipe away his soured disposition.

"What did my father say? Being at the right place at the right time makes all the difference in the world. Being in the wrong place never has a right time to be there."

He uncrossed his ankles and shrugged his tight shoulders. "Could use a massage right now," he mumbled. His shoulders and neck seemed to cramp up whenever he looked at the photos Molly had taken of him back then, and lovingly placed in the album. It revived the needling shame Jarvis felt he deserved, and the only way he could let Molly exact vengeance on him without her knowing. "Maybe I should have told you, I don't know," and peeked questioningly upward.

When he lowered his eyes, he tried to focus his attention just on Molly, and the pictures in front of him. "I do look pretty good in those running shorts. Not too skinny." He feigned a weak laugh. "Didn't have this," and he patted his thickened belly. "I probably should start walking," he told himself, and then spoke to Molly again.

"One of my disappointments has always been that you never went to any of the 5K runs, but you know that. If we hadn't argued, and you had gone to just that one race, I wouldn't have fallen prey to Joanna's wiles." Abruptly Jarvis pressed his face into one of resignation and shame. "Who am I kidding? It's not your fault, and not even hers. All mine. Even if my intent was completely innocent, I should have said no. I'm happily married! Happily."

Every time he mulled the scenario past the atoning reprimand of conventional wisdom, it ended with the same question. *Why did I let it go on? Simple answer, older guy found attractive by another woman. Steroids for the ego. But I should have cut it off right at the beginning. I wasn't looking for anybody. Molly and I had a great relationship. We did. Better than most.*

Jarvis flattened his brows as he tried to find a reason to refute his conclusion, and then thinking out loud, "But the truth is what it is. My judgement skewed because I was thinking about me, and not Molly. Not us." He shook his head, reluctantly accepting what had happened. "Sure, we were sometimes like two cantankerous engines getting started on a cold morning, but then, what marriage doesn't run rough occasionally?

We didn't argue much, grumble, yea, but bash each other over the head with spiteful comments. Nah. And when we did butt heads, it was mostly about silly stuff. "You didn't take the garbage out last night. Do you want us to get ants? For the millionth time, you don't wear dark socks with shorts!"

Jarvis sighed, longing for something that was lost, and knowing that cherished memories were the best he could hope for, even if some of them were painful. "I miss those verbal tussles of ours, Molly. You were right fifty, sixty percent of the time, probably more, but I'm a stubborn cuss. I don't like giving in or admitting I was wrong. You put up with a lot." Tears balanced precariously at the corners of his eyes, but only one or two rolled down his cheeks.

"Can't forget the sex. Most guys long for what we had." He chuckled in remembrance. "That was important to me, to us. The last two or three years, we were not exactly two squealing pigs, but before that. I will always have visions of you standing naked in the hallway after a hot shower, droplets of water still perched on your breasts and shoulders. Didn't take long for Freddy to stand at attention." A sliver of laughable recollection parted his lips. "You thought it was so funny that I would give my penis a name. Guess it is kind of crazy."

Jarvis rubbed his temples, hoping to massage away the sudden appearance of a headache, but there was no relief. *Just tension. Maybe if I lay down*, he thought. He rocked up and tramped to the bedroom, gently shaking his head, hoping that might oust the intrusive cobweb of the other woman's presence, but it only aggravated his pain. *Must set my alarm for supper.* Ten minutes later she still taunted him with guilt, but this time his eyes were closed, and he was beginning to snore.

Tabors had started filling up with the after-work crowd, and Jarvis was glad he had arrived early enough to get their table. "Our table," he remarked. "Our table? Not our table," he chided annoyedly. "This is the third, and last time. No more dalliance," he admonished. *Some mid-life crisis thing, and a seductive woman conniving to draw me into her trap. Not happening!* Near the end of their first meeting, she pressed him three times that they should meet again. That was the excuse for last week's tryst. Jarvis frowned affirmatively as he thought, *Today, just a quick drink, and I'm out of here. This is it!*

Curious though, because that had been the plan last Thursday, and he ended up being ensconced in flirtatious conversation that kept them there for two hours. Mostly idle talk, but permeated with enough suggestive repartees to tease out figments of inappropriate desires.

Molly and I have trouble talking for thirty minutes straight, he noted afterward. *After eighteen years, we know so much about each other, we can complete each other's sentences or thoughts. Amusing in the beginning, but it does become aggravating at times. Boring too.*

Now, looking toward the entrance, Jarvis could see Joanna's sprightly features bouncing toward him as she weaved in and around other customers. The sight of her wrangled with his emotions, and made his heart throb. But just as quickly, nagging contrition scoured his conscience with anxiety.

"Hello Joanna," he said in an affable, but noncommittal tone. He hoped the crinkles around his eyes would not make his greeting seem more welcoming than he intended.

"Hi baby," she said, and smudged a lingering kiss on his cheek before sitting down.

Uh oh. I'm in deep shit, Jarvis groaned silently, his apprehension hidden behind a forced smile. *A little too presumptuous on her part?*

"Good week?" she asked, peering expectantly at him, and signaling to the waitress collecting her tip one table over.

"Be there in a sec," she said.

Joanna was wearing a blouse with a floral design, and a hospitable peek at her decolletage.

Not a good start, Jarvis bemoaned, imagining his whole brain wincing in self conviction.

"Do you like them," Joanna asked teasingly after they had ordered wine and appetizers.

"What?" Jarvis asked.

"You've been staring at my chest since I sat down."

"Really? Oh, I'm sorry," he apologized, blushing. "I'm distracted. Lots on my mind." *And you're practically pushing them in my face.*

"Want to talk about it?"

"Uh, no. Little tired. Been busy with clients. I'll be fine." Already, Jarvis could feel himself surrendering to Joanna's hypnotic charm, and the soft mounds didn't hurt any either.

"So, today," she said vehemently, "I had a bird in my car. Must have squeezed in through the cracked windows. I thought I would have to call animal control, but as soon as the door opened, it flew out, tweeting like I was responsible for it being there. Have you ever had anything so unusual happen to you?" She edged forward, attentively caressing his floundering composure with her eyes.

"Uh, besides meeting an attractive woman at a 5K?"

Joanna reached out and touched his hand. "Yes, besides that you silly man." A voice that made Jarvis want to pull her across the table and kiss her hard on the lips.

Down boy. Down, he warned himself, and then speaking out loud, "Hmm, lots of unusual things happened to me through the years. Most of them my own doing." The line cajoled Joanna to gaze at him even more intently.

Jarvis squinched his forehead in deep concentration and pulled his hand away from the table to hold his chin. *Must be something I can talk about. Think!*

"I bet you have a trove of experiences to choose from," Joanna conjectured, and nodded with encouragement.

Seconds later, the waitress interrupted the swirl of mundane conversation, by serving drinks, and bringing the appetizers.

Jarvis absent mindedly watched her leave, and then felt the seductive pull from across the table. "So many moments to choose from, but now I know which one I'll tell you about," he said, deliberately returning Joanna's flattering attention. "Nineteen-ninety-four. June, I think. Been in Los Angeles for a Real Estate conference and was leaving the city for my late flight from LAX to Kennedy. I was tired and couldn't wait to snooze when I got on the plane. The windows were open slightly, the music was blasting, and I was sipping a cup of coffee."

"Wouldn't that keep you awake?"

"Not the way I was feeling. Besides, thought it better to reach the airport in one piece."

"Glad you did," Joanna murmured, a brief flush of pink coloring her face.

Now that's a reaction I wouldn't expect, Jarvis reflected. "Anyhow, it was about seven, and I began to notice the highway before me was mostly empty. It was the 405 and should have been packed at that hour. Vehicles were pulled over to the shoulder, and on the other side, traffic was practically stopped. People were standing along the meridian like they were waiting for a parade.

"This is peculiar," I thought. I pulled out the CD and glanced in the rearview mirror. There was a white, Ford Bronco approaching me, with a phalanx of police cars following behind. "Oh shit, what did I do wrong?" and angled the car over to the side. When none of those vehicles seemed to be slowing up, I realized something else was happening. I turned the radio on for the news and learned OJ was in that Bronco. I practically wrenched my neck twisting my head around to watch the parade pass by.

I saw his head, but it all happened so quickly, I can't be sure. The roof of my car was famous. You could see it on one of the videos that played over and over the next few days."

"Wow, an eyewitness," Joanna said flippantly. "I'm surprised you weren't subpoenaed for the trial."

"Who said I wasn't," Jarvis teased.

"You were not."

"I know. Who would need that kind of publicity?"

They reached for their wine at the same time, exchanging allusive smiles, and eyeing each other over sips of chardonnay. *Here I am, still acting like some infatuated teenager,* Jarvis groused silently. *Haven't mentioned Molly or the kids since out first meeting. And I'm beginning to think Joanna has an agenda, and I'm it. Miss innocent, trying to reel me in. I need to slam on the brakes.* He plowed his left hand through his hair, hoping she would be mindful of the golden band on his ring finger. "Quiet all of sudden," she said assailing him with an inquiring gaze that ignored the ring.

Making me nutso woman, Jarvis thought munching hurriedly on his shrimp appetizer. "Thinking about Molly, and the kids. We're going to the beach in two weeks. Probably the last time we all go together because Michael and Shelly are teenagers now and don't want their parents around." His demeanor brightened. *Reminded her I'm a family man. Better start acting like one.* Jarvis pushed back from the table, hoping a little more distance, even a foot, might let him better decipher Joanna's intentions, and reconsider his own. It didn't take him long to assign guilt. *Must be written all over my face,* he decided.

"No reason your wife should be upset with us. You're a loving and faithful husband."

Yep, faithful, Jarvis lectured silently. *How come I'm feeling guilty?*

Joanna tilted forward, letting the display of her breasts do some of the talking, "I was in a funk, and you helped pull me out of it. I know decent men exist because one of them is sitting at the table." She smiled with artful oblige.

Cunning like a fox, Jarvis noted cautiously. "Believe me, you, uh, offer men a lot."

Joanna lightly grasped his hand. "It's been a while since I felt this at ease around a man. I always believe they're trying to seduce me. Isn't that silly?"

Jarvis forced a cough. *Like I think you're trying to do with me.*

"I don't make you uncomfortable, do I?" she asked bluntly.

"No. No," Jarvis said waving off her prying concern.

"Because I want to see you again," Joanna finished. "Saturday? Four O'clock? Perhaps at my place this time. Half hour? Maybe an hour." Her eyes widened in prurient appeal, and her lips parted, the tip of the tongue licking them in lascivious invitation.

Jarvis struggled to keep his attention someplace, any place less provocative. *Jesus, help me*, his mind screeched. *I can't seriously consider her proposition.* His eyes flicked back to the libidinous temptation sitting across from him. "Just a half hour," he asserted with an air of false confidence and hidden reproach.

Joanna smiled at him. "Good. More relaxing without all these other people." She tacitly flicked them away with her hand and stood up. "I should have told you that I have a meeting in town. Besides, we can't spend too much time together or people will get the wrong idea."

Jarvis feigned a laugh. "Yea, that's right." and then grimaced as Joanna kissed him again, this time on the forehead.

"Looking forward to Saturday," she flirted winking at him.

"Oh God," he groaned watching her walk away. "Why did I give in?!"

This burden of complicity was tugging on his conscience when the alarm startled him awake. "What the... who, what," he brayed exploring the night table with his hand and finally whacking the dismiss icon on his phone. The headache seemed less, but she was still there.

The pillow beneath him was warm and moist, and he flipped it over to the cool, dry side. "Better," he murmured, and then frowned at the illumined time glaring back at him. "Not hungry," he grumped. "Got to chase that woman out of my head and get back to sleep. Just close my eyes and think good thoughts. That's what Molly would say." But the dream loitered like a vagrant in his brain even as somnolence began to pull him back into its normally consoling arms. Except tonight there was a storm brewing, and it didn't provide him with any comfort.

Jarvis was sitting calmly in his car, staring vacantly out the windshield, a combination of trepidation and commonsense stopping him from opening the door. If someone had passed by, the person might have shouted, "Hey mister," just to be sure the mannequin took a breath and moved. *Can't believe I've been so stupid to let the past four weeks come to this. Why didn't I listen to that little voice in my head?* Jarvis tapped the steering wheel nervously and sighed. *It's like playing a game of Russian roulette. You challenging me God? Think I'll be drawn into Miss Innocent's snare? I'll prove to you how strong I am.*

He stared balefully out the window at the passing clouds. *We've been baiting each other for weeks,* he admitted *and a couple times, I've let my imagination run wild.* His countenance scrunched determinedly as he tried holding fast to the foreboding guilt that momentarily stomped down his libido, but instead he let himself fall prey to his desire to see the woman once again.

Jarvis knocked three times before the door opened. Joanna was wearing the black running shorts she wore when they first met, mid-thigh, and adhering to every crease. A hot pink sports bra tucked in her breasts but didn't hide the imprint of her nipples.

I could play ring toss on those, Jarvis thought. "Uh, hi," he managed to say.

"Oh, hi," she said with a lilt of enthusiastic surprise. "I didn't think you would show, appeared a little unsure of yourself the other day, so I was getting ready to run. Guess I need to throw something over these clothes."

For some reason I have my doubts about that story, Jarvis thought warily.

"Looks like you could use a drink," she continued, attempting to suppress a few leaked giggles with her hand.

"I'm alright," Jarvis asserted. *Jeez, you're an invitation to trouble,* he thought.

Joanna smiled beguilingly. "Where are my manners. Come inside. I'll get drinks for both of us." She turned, and he followed her seductive wiggle down a short hallway.

"*Mm, nice legs,*" he observed with unfettered lust. He smacked his temple. *Think I just crossed the River Styx.*

"Have a seat in the living room," she shouted from the kitchen. "Be there in a minute."

"Ok," he replied quietly. "Make it a ginger ale." He didn't hear any response. *Maybe you should do an about face and walk right out of here,* his conscience earnestly suggested. *Not yet*, Jarvis argued back. He sat in a flowery armchair for safety and rubbed his lips anxiously. "Enough space between me and that sofa," he mumbled.

He gazed around the room like it was a potential crime scene, and he was going be the victim. *Joanna, uh, I don't even know her last name*, he thought inconceivably, *with the candlestick, in the living room.* Jarvis chuckled. He and Molly used to play the board game with Michael and Shelly five or six times a year. No candlestick, but there were a couple of table lamps.

"There you are," Joanna said striding into the room. "Your drink sir."

"Uh, thanks." he replied, noting she had just slipped into a checkered, button down shirt that was still open in the front. *Still loaded for bear I see*, Jarvis observed. *Glad I'm over here!*

Joanna sat down on the sofa and crossed her legs, which pulled the spandex further up her thigh. "Let's drink," she insisted raising her glass.

"Good idea. My throat is a little dry." After taking a sip, Jarvis's eyes squinched as he looked past her legs and into the expectant face. "This certainly isn't ginger ale."

A coy smile greeted his disclosure. "Thought something stronger might be better. Relax any inhibitions."

"My inhibitions keep me safe," he returned, although with more wit than reproof. "Did I tell you about the time I was robbed?" he asked, hoping to distract his opponent, and relieve some of the tension twisting in his chest.

"No."

"It was about twenty years ago. Wow, twenty years, shortly before I ran into Molly," and embraced the memory with a loving smile, *Good way to remind Joanna I'm married. Me too.* "It was dark, and I had just come home from a date. I lived in a townhouse then, and pulling in, noticed the upstairs light was on. I couldn't recall using it earlier in the day, so I opened the front door cautiously, and shouted, "Glad I'm home." Jackets and coats were strewn all over the floor, but nothing else seemed to be disturbed. However, I did notice in the kitchen that the window over the sink was open. I grabbed an umbrella, and yelled upstairs, "I'm coming up!"

Joanna giggled. "An umbrella?"

"Well, I could practice some fencing," Jarvis offered, meekly acknowledging it was a harebrained ploy. "Anyway, didn't hear any footsteps, so I crept up slowly, and checked all the rooms. Clothes all over the place. The only thing missing was a big jar of coins. Someone desperate for money, I guess. The police never did find out who did it."

"You must have been scared."

"A little perhaps, but adrenaline was pumping, and I was angry."

"The macho side of you, huh? Why don't you come over here," Joanna suggested enticingly, and patted the cushions beside her. She tucked her legs beneath her and took an excruciatingly deep breath that seemed to pull the material tighter against her breasts.

Just for me, Jarvis thought flippantly. The suspect invitation a slap to his head to wake up. "I don't think so. I'm comfortable here."

"Don't you trust me?" she asked. "I'm hurt."

"It's not you. It's me. Be better if we kept a little space between us."

"Jarvis, I can't believe you said that. Now come over here."

"Uh, I don't think so," he answered. *I can't. I can't*, kept echoing in his head. "If I sat over there, I, uh"

"What would happen?" she purred seductively.

Jarvis stood up with herculean effort. "I don't know, and I don't want to know," he argued, brandishing the words as a moat of protection. *Missed opportunity*, the lustful animal in him whispered. *No! Be strong!* his rational side argued, and then it all spilled out of him. "Joanna, I've enjoyed our time together, but it was only supposed to be that one occasion. This whole situation has gone way past celebrating your second place finish." He looked grievously at Joanna who was eyeing him with either curiosity or suspicion or both, he couldn't tell.

"I…"

"No!" he said cutting her off. I love Molly. I love being married to her. I can't do this anymore." With that, he turned around and walked quickly out of the room.

CHAPTER ELEVEN

Jarvis seldom had visitors drop in anymore. Michael and Shelly stopped by two or three times a week to say hello, but they were family, and that was different. *Checking up on me is what they're doing, he surmised.* Yet there was nothing like old friends to share old stories. One couple had moved to Florida, however that was like a slow death because over time the communication got less and less, and Molly was the one who had done any face book time with them. Ed Michaels, a buddy from the service, moved near his children in Ohio. *Makes sense at our age. Guess that's why I'm still living here,* Jarvis reasoned. *"Besides, the satisfaction of having the kids wait on me after all these years. Bout time."* He shook his head indulgently, and smirked.

The last two people in their former close, knit group, lived within ten miles, but spent every day trying to figure out who the person was in the mirror. "Scares the crap out of me," Jarvis had said on more than one occasion.

So, he was taken aback when his brother-in-law, Ken Bonet dropped in early one morning.

"That French?" he had asked Molly on their first real date, the one after having their smashing introduction.

"How astute of you" she had replied, with playful sassiness.

"I can be rather intuitive."

"I'll be the judge of that."

Anyhow, his brother-in-law had arrived with no call. No messages. Just, "Here I am."

"Don't you read your texts," Ken practically scolded. He was thinner now, and there was a gentle curve to his spine.

"Text? I never got one from you."

His brother-in-law scowled. "Must have sent it to the wrong number."

Kind of sparse on the top, too, Jarvis noted after they sat down. *And if I was a betting man, those pearly whites probably soak in a container at night. I just have to take my bottoms out,* he thought triumphantly. "My God, how long has it been Ken? Two, three years?"

"Been since Molly died two years ago." He struggled to throw back his shoulders and sit straight.

"Oh yea," Jarvis said quietly. "I remember you at the Memorial service. Consoling words. You said your sister lived a very fulfilling life, and you thanked me for making her happy."

There was a residual silence which neither man filled with an opening line, so Jarvis used the moment to bask in the number of people who had shown up to pay their respects, and all the nice comments they made. *Teachers touch so many lives,* he reflected resolutely.

When Ken still didn't say anything, Jarvis began to fidget in his seat, and rub his temples. Unexpected gaps in conversation made him uneasy. *Hell, we haven't seen each other in two years, he should have something to say. Guess I should too,* he thought, frowning. "Uh, Ken, where is the boss?" he finally asked.

The man sighed and raised his eyebrows as if nervously searching for an answer. "She's up there," he said thumbing towards the ceiling. "Four months ago. Probably playing bridge with Molly right now and pissed off I left her alone again."

"Oh. Sorry. Didn't know." Jarvis offered apologetically. *Surprised he didn't tell me when it happened. Guess we've gotten estranged from each other.*

Ken shrugged his shoulders, as if begrudgingly saying, we all go sometime. "She could be overbearing occasionally, but for some reason I loved her. It was the little things, making my lunch for work, making sure the house was clean... hmm, not so little a task with me around." A semblance of a grin etched on his face. "She gave great backrubs. Laying cement all day is tough on the body." A passing haplessness seemed to weigh down on him, sinking his voice, and texturing his face with weariness.

Jarvis could identify with the demeanor but confessing he had experienced such feelings after Molly's passing would have embarrassed them both. *Just not manly.*

"Miss the old girl, but don't tell her."

"Implying I'm going first?" Jarvis joked.

"Just in case you do," Ken answered, dutifully jettisoning his despondency.

Jarvis chuckled. "I'd make a bet with you, but don't want to jinx myself. So, what brings you back to town?"

"On the way to visit my son. Thought I'd swing over and see if you were home. He told me the whole trip was too much for me, and I shouldn't drive. Getting old. Hah." They both chortled and shared the same look of scoffing acknowledgement.

"Shelly told me the other day I was too old to push mow the lawn. I advised her it was great exercise. Course she wasn't satisfied with that answer. It does take me longer though."

"Don't most things take longer," Ken observed facetiously. "Well, my Dave is a manager at Walmart. Guess he'll never have to worry about losing his job unless he mucks up big time. Don't like the girl he's dating now. Too many tattoos, and one kid." He raised his eyebrows, and splayed out his hands. "Just want him to be happy."

"Happiness cannot be overrated," Jarvis agreed. "Michael and Shelly have good jobs too. Mike's divorced, and Shelly had several "*all hands-on deck*", sessions with her husband, and a counselor. Think they are doing okay. Guess we did pretty good, huh?" Ken nodded, as Jarvis barged ahead. "Look a little pale. You alright these days?"

His brother-in-law leaned back as best he could, and harrumphed. "Medicine I'm on. Supposed to stay out of the sun as much as possible. Did not anticipate being caged in a house when I got older. I sneak out to play golf on the cloudy days."

Poor guy. So bent over. Don't know how he can see over the dash, or play golf, Jarvis thought. Wouldn't *want to be on the road with him.*

"So, how you are feeling?" Ken asked, then chuckling, added, "God, guess we are getting older if we're talking about our medical problems."

"Like it should be part of our everyday conversation," Jarvis cracked flippantly. He shrugged his shoulders. "Eh. Somedays I feel like I should be put up on a lift, and have my undercarriage checked, and my tires rotated. Today is not bad. Hey, you want something to eat or drink... a peanut butter and jelly sandwich?"

"No thanks. Can't stay too long," a tainted voice answered, one now infected with the hint of annoyance.

Jarvis immediately peered at Ken, uncertain what was wrong. *His mood changes faster than Molly's indecision on what to wear. Was it something I said?*

"Know what bothers me, Jarvis?" his brother-in-law grumbled, inclining forward and commandeering Jarvis's total attention. "Four months are gone, and I figure it would be acceptable to sneak glances at some of the ladies, ten, twenty years younger. Try to get their attention. Been wondering if they'd go out with me. Free meal. No expectations. Just someone to sit with and share stories.

But the other day, some woman called me a lecher. Says it's despicable what I'm doing. Said I was leering. I wasn't leering. And it's not like they're teenagers." He rested a few moments, before harassing Jarvis again with his harangue. "What happened to the day when a man could look at a female, and try to make some eye contact? And yet," he emphasized, "it's okay for a cougar to gawk at some young guy and remark how good his ass looks. Sounds like a double standard to me."

Jarvis guffawed at the man's predicament. He imagined him hiding behind trees or ducking into alleys like he was Inspector Clouseau following a suspect. "Different world. Different generation Ken. I'm surprised you're not doing one of those online dating services."

"Nah. Too many people lie. What you see and read isn't what you get. Some of them actually download a photo of someone else."

"Really? Well, you'd probably tell them you're six feet, and have a full head of hair. Besides, younger women are looking for someone with a heartbeat," Jarvis joked.

"They could put their ear to my chest anytime," his brother-in-law spouted cockily. It made Jarvis snort with amusement.

"You know Ken, in my two years alone, I never considered looking for someone else. There's only one Molly. Maybe your quarry should be a little bit older."

Ken crossed his arms defensively and grumped. "Let me tell you something Jarvis, we're not dead yet. Besides, I just expect something platonic."

"Well, if you can keep it that way, maybe it'll work," Jarvis replied, not believing his own advice. "Platonic didn't work for me forty-one years ago. Ended up with two children."

Ken glanced around, and then craned his neck forward as if the room was full of nosey guests. "At our age, we should have nothing to hide from each other." He paused. "Now a days, I would need scaffolding to hold the damn thing up. Acts more like a wilted flower. That Viagra only worked for a couple years."

Jarvis laughed so hard his face turned red, and a trickle of pee moistened his shorts. "Sorry Ken, but the way you said it," he demurred hoping to repair the imprudent response. *"So funny, but true,"* he admitted with embarrassed silence.

His brother-in-law was grinning like he had been practicing the joke for weeks, but soon his features were shadowed in unamused impatience when Jarvis continued with another spatter of chuckles.

"Alright, alright," Ken said frowning, and waving away any more convulsive responses. When Jarvis appeared composed, he asked, "So, who do you think is going to be the best team in the NFL East this year?"

"They're going to have a best team?" was the sputtered reply.

"Funny. I forgot you were a contrarian. Suppose I shouldn't ask what you think about the President either."

"You know I'm an independent, but if I were to name a few things, demagog, pathological liar, narcissist come to mind."

"Are you kidding," Ken said crossing his arms.

"Uh, not open to a civil discussion, huh? Okay," Jarvis demurred. *Certainly not worthy of an argument.*

"Hear about that virus in China?"

"Yea. Hope it stays over there. Maybe the President can put a tariff on that."

"Huh, what did you say," Ken asked. "Sometimes I don't hear things exactly right. Probably need my hearing checked.

"Too bad we can't put a tariff on that!" Jarvis declared. He expected Ken to rebut his comment, but the man just nodded, apparently ignoring the subtle sarcasm. *"And another reason not to be on the road with you,"* Jarvis reflected. *"Be nice to know you can hear someone beeping their horn."*

"But I still say we needed those taxes to punish China for its unfair trade practices." his brother-in-law continued.

"Here we go again," Jarvis quietly groused, wrangling with the opportunity to repeat his argument that tariffs were bad policy. *Why don't people realize when we buy another country's products, the additional costs are tacked on at American ports. It's the consumer who ends up getting stiffed.* "No comment," he finally said.

Ken apparently took this as a victory, because he peeked at his watch, and stood up in a slow, grinding motion.

Move like that myself when the weather is bad, Jarvis thought, and *sometimes when it's not bad.*

"Time to go." his brother-in-law said. "Dave will be sending the State Police after me if I don't show up on time. Won't that be an embarrassment." He sighed and stuck out his hand. "For two old guys, think we're doing alright." He stopped, and momentarily seemed to ponder the floor for his next comment. "And I'll take you up on your suggestion to date women my own age. Not exactly prime choice anymore." He swept a hand over the glistening top of his head and smiled. "Hey, glad I stopped by."

"Me too. Have to keep in touch," Jarvis said earnestly, though it was more of a reflexive response to be cordial. *Doubt we'll see each other again, except perhaps if the casket is open.*

Later that afternoon, he was reminiscing about Molly and what made her so special. Maybe it was the way he could teasingly annoy her and provoke a reaction, like when he used toilet paper to blow his nose. "What are you doing? That's for wiping your butt. Do you know how many germs have jumped off the last person's hands or leap frogged from the toilet seat? "Then she would roll her eyes and extend her fingers in exasperation. *She could be funny that way*, he thought with wry approval.

Naturally, that gave Molly license to curve ball him in return. One time she announced that if he died first, she might consider getting married again, or maybe just live with a man. "Be good to experience someone different after all these years," his wife said with a mask of sincerity.

"You would do that?" Jarvis asked, surprised, and as he told her later, a tiny bit hurt."

"Mm..., maybe not," she replied with a secretive smile. "One man is enough, and turning, left him trying to reconcile her with someone else.

I would be dead. What would be the big deal? What if he was larger than me?

The rest of the day, flashes of Molly kept reminding him how blessed he had been to have her in his life. She had spritzed those thirty-nine years together with an indelible passion, and a certain Joie de vivre. Suddenly a soft, loving chuckle gurgled up like the effervescent popping of a Champaigne cork when a scene of unforgiving frustration turned into one of humiliation and sensual desire.

Humorous now perhaps, but not then, Jarvis thought. *It certainly humbled my male ego.* An electric can opener had been getting the best of him, and a conspiratorial wife had been watching her hapless husband from one corner of the kitchen.

"Son of a bitch opener," he muttered watching the can of vegetables spin around for the third time. "This isn't funny guys," he carped at the beans, as if expecting some semblance of sympathy. "Must be broken."

"Won't open, huh?" a bemused voice said behind him.

"Huh. Oh. Didn't know you were there," he said with high pitched surprise, and a jump of his shoulders. "No! It must be broken." He growled.

"Here, let me try," Molly said, confidently marching over, and grabbing the can. "You do it like this," shoving it up, and into the cutting blade while she held down the handle.

"Course it's going to work now," he murmured.

"There, that's how you do it," Molly said, proudly displaying the lid in one hand and the opened can in the other.

"Luck." Jarvis uttered with a hint of playful malice.

"Really?" she said grabbing another one from the cabinet, and successfully removing the top off it too. A smug satisfaction settled on her face.

"Think you're so smart," he said with a twinge of libidinous revenge welling up inside him. "So, what are you going to do with two opened cans of beans?"

"Not sleep under the same covers with you tonight. And what's that expression on your face? What are you planning?" his wife asked with timid anticipation. "I've got two cans of beans in my hands, mister. I don't want to dump them over your head." He blocked her way of escape and backed her gently against the counter, "Now Jarvis," she threatened weakly. "You behave yourself."

"Oh, I will," he said mimicking the voice of Count Dracula. "Give me a kiss," and laid a wet nibble on the side of her neck. He easily pried the vegetables from her hands and put then on the counter behind her. "You make me crazy," Jarvis said in a hammed up carnal tone.

Molly made a halfhearted effort to writhe away, but he held her firmly against his body, lazily dragging his fingers up and under the hem of her dress.

"Not fair," Molly murmured, playing along with his fantasy.

When he touched the warm material between her legs, she held him closer for support.

"I've got you now, woman," Jarvis murmured with lascivious intent.

"You're bad. Very, very bad," she groaned, as if reading his mind. Then dropping an arm down and feeling the front of his pants. "And a very bad little boy!"

When the distraction of their amorous tomfoolery gradually faded, Jarvis proudly noticed a small bulge down below. *Like earning a merit badge after sixty-five,* he thought. Then he grabbed his chin between index and thumb and adopted a more solemn expression. *Would have been forty-one years. Miss the companionship and her being there in the morning when I roll over. But I have no desire to get tangled up with another woman. Been down that road and learned my lesson. Wish Ken all the luck in the world.*

That night, a dream swooped in, and disrupted Jarvis's plan for an unspoiled, restful sleep. Periodically, it would let him escape from its grasp, and his thoughts would momentarily flounder for some haven before being yanked back in. One time he awoke to pee and was hard as a rock. "*Wow, three times in a month! I'm on a roll!*" And then with a cynical smile, he murmured, "Molly use to say men's lives revolve around their penis."

"That's not true," he would argue. "Family, job, and beliefs are more important."

"Yes, they are," she would reply with a smirk.

"My God, I've got to get home right away," Jarvis yelled frantically from the depths of his repose. It was nine O'clock in the morning on September, eleventh, two thousand and one, and he was picking up two sixteen-inch chains for his chainsaw. Outside, the air was a comfortable fifty degrees, jacket weather, and serene with birds whistling, and squirrels bounding over grass that needed cutting. But inside the store, two other men were silently watching a television sitting high above them on a shelf behind the counter. Their faces were gaunt.

"Some kind of disaster movie?" Jarvis asked, innocently joining the group.

"No movie," one of the men said. "This is real. A passenger jet crashed into one of the towers about fifteen minutes ago."

"Jeez, that's horrible," Jarvis murmured, peering at the screen.

Abruptly a strident voice announced another plane headed toward the skyscrapers, and seconds later, all the men shouted, "Shit!" as a jet plowed into the other tower.

"Oh my god!" Jarvis gasped. "We're under attack." He could feel his heart pounding and his breathing quicken. His fingers tingled, and the floor felt momentarily uneven beneath him. Grabbing the counter, he steadied himself, and tried to salvage whatever composure wasn't being devoured by metastasizing dread. *Get the chains later. Got to get home to Molly.*" He turned around and ran to the truck as fast as his shaky legs allowed, terrified what he would hear or see next. "My God, I've got to get home right away," he exclaimed, banging the top of his head as he leaped into the truck, and behind the steering wheel. "Molly must be hysterical. Got to get to her!"

The tires spit gravel as Jarvis jammed his foot down on the gas pedal. *Jeez, I can't believe this! I want her in my arms!*" a prayerful plea cried out. A pall of desperation and fear fell upon him, and flaunted unsafe speeds, and expletives when anyone got in front of him. The anxiety seemed to pin his breath inside him and only began to lift when he braked hard turning into their driveway. Molly was outside, pale, trembling, and breathing in short, shallow breaths. The voice of a radio played in the background.

"Did you?"

"I did," Jarvis said, hugging Molly like he hadn't seen her in a year.

"I'm so glad you're here," she whimpered. "I love you." She nestled deeply in his arms.

"I love you too baby. I may not stop holding you for a long time." "*God, I'm so glad I have this woman,*" Jarvis thought with fervent conviction.

Suddenly an urgent voice blared out, "Washington is on alert. A third plane has just crashed into the Pentagon." And moments later, a hollow groaning, that a fourth jet had been hijacked and might also be headed towards D.C.

Jarvis squeezed Molly tighter, and then released her. "I need a drink of water. My throat is dry," he croaked.

Molly tittered anxiously. "Mine too," she said.

In the cool of the late afternoon, after the morning's insanity, the passage of time allowed the dissembling appearance of calm to come over Jarvis as he walked hand in hand with his wife around the neighborhood. It was as if their fingers were knotted together so that nothing could tear them apart. "Makes me realize how fragile life is," he murmured. "And thankful for all the years we've had together."

"I know," Molly said leaning her head against his shoulder. "The kids. The grandkids. I want them to experience what we have."

"Yea," Jarvis replied wistfully. "Never thought we'd be concerned about an attack on our own soil."

"I know. Other places, but not here. Perhaps we have it too good in this country and take it all for granted."

"You might be right," Jarvis answered pulling Molly around in front of him. He caressed the side of her face and absorbed the questioning stare. "I love you," he whispered for the thousandth time.

CHAPTER TWELVE

At the end of Jarvis's street was a dirt path leading to a public playground. Many days, it seemed the set of swings, monkey bars, and two slides must have included a bunch of boisterous children with their delivery. The shorter slide was the length of Jarvis's outstretched body. He knew this because on a day the park was empty, he had laid down on it to get a quick tan.

"It's too hot," Molly warned him. "You're going to get burns lying on it without your shirt!" It was like she had tossed down the gauntlet, and he vowed to lay on the searing metal for as long as possible, just to prove a point. "You're crazy Jarvis Heath," she yelled at him.

"But a good crazy," he volleyed back.

The doctor gave him a cream and said apply it for a week to all the areas that were painfully red and blistered. Molly never did say, "I told you so." Instead, he had to endure her smirking expression, and "Oh, it must hurt so much," whenever she spread the lotion on his back and shoulders. But that was thirty-five years ago, when he was young, and risks were viewed as challenges, and not demonstrations of foolhardiness.

In the last years of her life, before she got sick, he would push Molly on a swing in that very same park. Sentimental moments spent together with silly talk, laughter, and youthful indiscretions, as much as their creaking bodies, and senescent modesty would let them get away with.

Today it had taken him about fifteen minutes to reach the playground and sit down on one of its benches. "No huffing or puffing. That's good," Jarvis asserted blithely. "Cooler than yesterday." He craned his head back and scanned the sky. "Cirrus, few cumulous, on a blanket of deep blue."

Jarvis closed his eyes and relished the sudden puff of wind caressing his face. *"Perfect day after last night's storm."*

There was still a helter-skelter design of large puddles in the play area from the rain, and the bench beneath him required blotting so he had somewhere to rest his thin-fleshed, old body. He wore a Niagra Falls cap to cover his sun blotched scalp and a worn, Five-K shirt from one of his first races.

"Won't be many here with all that water," he remarked. "Should be very peaceful."

And then, as if on cue, a young man with two energetic boys showed up. *"Five and six,"* Jarvis guessed.

They were screaming and yelling with excitement, hopping up and down like two rabbits in a field of clover, until they noticed all the water on the playground. Then the boys stiffened in horror, and their trumpeting glee became pitched exclamations of disappointment.

"Daddy, look at all the water," the taller one yelled.

"Don't worry," the father said calmly. "Take your shoes and socks off, and roll up your pants. Excitedly, the boys listened, flinging shoes and socks, and charging into the puddles.

"Mister, mind if I sit down?"

"No. Sit. The bench is dry now. Let me scoot over."

Jarvis gave the man the once over. "Looks in good shape. Athletic. Late twenties, early thirties," he surmised.

The father offered his hand. "My name is Randy. I have the boys this weekend, for another two hours," he said glancing at his watch. "Trial separation." He flicked his attention back to his sons, whose splashing seemed to have distracted their cheerless disposition.

"Doesn't sound thrilled about that separation business," Jarvis noted silently. "Few grays in those eyebrows. Guessing he colors the hair on top. Got a lot more than me."

"Thanks again for the seat, sir."

Jarvis laughed. "Been a long time since someone addressed me as sir. You military?"

"Four years army."

Jarvis acknowledged the response with a tacit shake of his head, and then surprised himself with a smile. "Two years ago, a doctor called me sir while he had me bending over for the proverbial finger up the butt."

"Huh?"

"Prostate thing. Don't worry, your turn is coming. Anyhow, after he completed the whole physical, he told me my prostate was benignly large, and don't be too concerned about it because a lot of old men have the same problem. Didn't like the old man crack, or the don't be too concerned about it remark. Felt insulted and questioned his advice. It's my body. I found another doc."

The younger man's expression reminded Jarvis of Molly's when he gave her street directions, and she had this baffled, what are you saying look in her eyes. *Thank God for GPS.*

Jarvis grinned. "Sorry. After I turned sixty-five, I started talking a lot and still don't know when to shut-up."

"Eh, don't worry about it," Randy said waving away the apology. He looked intently at Jarvis. "If you wouldn't mind, maybe you could give me some advice."

"Depends upon the subject. But I'll give it a shot."

"Talking to the guys at work about the separation, they think I should just suck it up, get the divorce when it's time, and be done with it. Not that easy." He sighed with what sounded like despair, and then stared contemplatively at his sons. "I miss her. I love her."

"Hmm, how long you two been together?"

"Eight years."

"You both still talking to each other?"

"Funny about that. Actually, seem to be getting along better."

"Have you seen a counselor?"

"Reason we're doing this separation," Randy continued. "I didn't think it was a good idea, but Patty said if that was the recommendation, maybe we should try it." He rubbed his chin pensively and glanced toward the squeals of exuberance. "Love those guys."

"I can understand why. Have two of my own, your age though, and now grandkids."

Jarvis hesitated before he proceeded. *Suppose the guy could tell me to "F" off. What the hell.* "So, what's the problem between you and your wife?"

"Me."

Jarvis cocked his head sideways, surprised by the answer and amazed by the honesty. *That's a positive start.*

"Hey dad, this is so much fun!" the shorter boy abruptly shouted.

Randy grinned. "Looks like it. Your skin is going to get all wrinkly," he teased. "Pants going to be soaked too. Oh well, something your mother will have to deal with after she berates me," he murmured resignedly.

He turned his head, and ignoring the impugning conjecture, slipped back into the conversation "Work. Overtime. Trying to get ahead. Golf on the weekends."

"Sound like a busy man," Jarvis noted. "Uh, any room in there for Patty or the boys?"

Randy shifted his weight around as if he was uncomfortable and momentarily strayed his eyes to the ground. "*Uh oh, trouble*," Jarvis thought.

"It's more like having to squeeze them into my schedule. I don't give them the attention they deserve. That's why I'm the problem. Take them for granted. Patty says I live like a bachelor."

"Hmm. Is she right?"

Randy's head bobbed affirmatively up and down like a buoy. "Yea."

"Seems to me a solution is staring you in the face."

"I think you're right and need to get my priorities straight." The man glanced at Jarvis's wedding band. "How long have you been married?"

"This year would make forty-one. Molly passed two years ago."

"Oh. Sorry."

Jarvis touched his ring, and then looked up. "Never find another one like her."

"How'd you do it?" Randy earnestly asked.

"No simple answer." Jarvis said leaning back and studying his pupil. *Hmm, where to start? I know.* "Think of marriage like a sport... maybe golf. Something that needs lots of practice to hone your skills. Time alone with your wife. I mean like dating, holding hands and laughing together. Avoid the sand traps as best you can. When there are arguments, one of you has got to yell "fore", before any shouting gets out of hand." He paused to let the message sink in, hoping it all made sense. "Not a golfer myself, afraid I'd spend all day on one hole." Randy grinned. Then Jarvis went on, "I know this sounds corny, but I used to leave little love notes around the house. Once I bought her a stuffed animal, put it behind the steering wheel while she was at work, and gave it a message, "Hey lady, there's a guy at home who says he's hungry for your body, mind and soul. He thinks you're special." Pretty effective."

"Think I get you," Randy replied with a subtle nod of his head. He leveled his eyes with Jarvis. "When I drop the boys off, I'm going to ask her out on a dinner date. We can talk about changes I want to make because she and the boys are, well, everything to me."

"Sounds like a start," Jarvis agreed. "Now, why don't you join your sons and kick the water around with them. They would love you for that. And when they inevitably tell their mother what you did, she might think it was pretty cool too."

"Thank you," Randy said, extending his hand. The clasp between them cementing a mutual respect. "Let me pull these sneakers off and get my feet wet."

"Good luck," Jarvis said.

After lunch, the hopefulness of the morning still animated Jarvis's spirits, and coaxed the memory of a similar situation to temporarily push aside any idea he had of taking a nap. The warmth it generated crooked a smile across his face and highlighted the *happy crinkles* around his eyes as Molly used to call them.

A veil of dismay hung over Michael and Shelly as they stared out the living room window at the rain which seemed to purposely loiter over the house and spoil any chance to play outside.

Ten and twelve, too young to be punished like this. They look so miserable, Jarvis thought looking up from the newspaper. *School all week, and now stuck inside on a Saturday. Maybe I can help.* He got up and stealthily crept down the hall. Molly was still cleaning one of the bathrooms, and then she was going to vacuum the upstairs. He had offered to help, but she had looked at him with one raised brow, as if to say, "I've seen your work."

"Kids, let's go outside," he suggested in a hushed tone.

Shelly giggled. "But daddy, it's raining."

Jarvis shrugged away the sensible response. "It's only water. We can splash in the puddles with our feet. We just have to roll up our jeans."

"I don't want to get wet," Michael complained.

"I'll get an umbrella and hold it over our heads."

"Won't mom get mad?"

"Maybe, but guess who will be the one really in trouble."

"You dad?" Michael answered disbelievingly.

Jarvis nodded. "So, let's try to keep it our secret." He glanced ruefully at Shelly as she slapped a hand over her mouth to cover up another gush of giggles. *"Yea, I'm in trouble already."* he thought.

A few minutes later, with the rain tapping persistently on the umbrella, they crept over to a large puddle on the lawn. "Now be serious," Jarvis teased, even as a barrage of laughter assailed his ears. He bent his knees, and said, "On three. One. Two. Three." And they all jumped together.

Michael purposely kicked some water in his father's direction. "I'll get you," Jarvis shouted, slapping the puddle with his foot. Shelly was screaming joyfully, ignoring the rain which spattered across her face, and jumping up and down, splashing water in all directions.

Grinning like a little boy catching the last out of the ballgame, Jarvis looked up at the house. "Uh, oh," he muttered. Molly stood in the window, shaking her finger at him. But as he continued to stare at her, he noticed she seemed to be having difficulty suppressing a smile. "Only one year hard labor," he thought.

CHAPTER THIRTEEN

"This year is turning out to be rather crappy," Jarvis remarked bitterly between deep breaths. "The body is finally giving in. Afraid I can't pretend I'm forty anymore." He glanced up pleadingly. "How about a truce? Extend the shelf life a few years?"

He took a long gulp of water that left him a little breathless, but no worse than he had been two minutes before when he had finished push mowing the small patch of lawn he called a yard. *Probably shouldn't drink so much at one time, but I'm parched.*

Shelly had yelled at him for doing too much about two weeks ago and two weeks before that.

"It's good exercise," he had protested.

"Daddy, you're seventy-five years old. Working outside in this heat is not good for you. You can pay someone to do the property or have Michael do it."

"You hurt my feelings Shelly," Jarvis had said looking askance at her and shaking his head in disappointment. "If I don't keep myself busy, I'll seize up like an engine."

The angst he experienced was like the short-lived resentment he felt when Molly's addiction to her phone and social media almost befouled their relationship. "That was another crappy year," he bemoaned, "or at least those first few months." A timely, tap dance of guilt reminded him that many years before, it had been an indiscretion of his own doing that almost snapped the bonds of the marriage. So, who was he to be judge and jury?

Jarvis figured it was a communist plot. At least that's what he surmised when the cellphone, smartphone, I-pad, and the whole smorgasbord of social media infiltrated society so easily and became so indispensable. Driving. Walking. Dating. Board meetings. Bedtime lover. Yes, even bedtime lover. It made Jarvis sick.

He would have to admit that even he felt momentarily uneasy if the phone was accidently left at the house. *What if one of the kids need me, or worse, I drive into a deep ravine, and my only means of getting help is sitting in my drawer at home?* Graciously, after fifteen seconds of this trumped up panic, he would roll his eyes shamefully, and scold the reflection in the rearview mirror. *For most of my life, the closest I ever got to a cell was watching Kirk use his Communicator on Star Trek. I think I can survive a trip into town.*

Then inevitably he would pass another vehicle whose driver would have their head bowed as if in prayer. "They're going to need some prayer if they keep driving like that," Jarvis sarcastically muttered. "What happened to the days when a message was written on a piece of paper, or blinking on some machine?" He tilted his head backward at the red light. "Wonder if they've got this problem in Heaven?" He let his imagination get the best of him, again.

Gabriel, I need you.

Uh, can you wait a minute Lord. Just want to finish this session.

Wait a minute? God thundered. Give me that!

I'm playing "Beat the Devil at his own Game. It's very intriguing. Probably help the freshman angels learn the routine.

The recruits will learn as they always have since the beginning of time, from the blackboard, and rote!

Jarvis smirked, but the joke was on him, and he knew it. The very thing he deplored in others had intruded into his own home and ensnared his wife with its willful seduction. It was an addiction that metastasized out of control and tested the steel of the marriage.

"Molly was sixty-four! Sixty-four!" He still had trouble believing it sometimes. The obsession handcuffed her ability to manage its presence in her life. She had an umbilical need for social media, Facebook, Instagram, and all the rest of it. It controlled her waking hours, and impeded sleeping ones. She was even sucked into the scintillating bribery of twenty-four hour news that she frequently complained had become too depressing.

"So why watch it?"

"I don't want to miss anything, and you're out on the road. What if something important happens, or some emergency announcement flashes across the screen?"

"Like a meteorite is going to hit the earth." Jarvis responded dryly. She would sigh like he was a hopeless case and look away.

They had been married almost thirty-five years, and he had never seen her caught up in such craziness. And the fact that so many others had fallen prey to its fawning enticement did not provide Jarvis with any solace. This was his wife, and he wanted her back.

He shifted his position in the lounge chair, and tugged on his upper lip, which he subconsciously did when a situation's obtrusiveness taunted his understanding and control. Jarvis still believed a sinister force had been at play, conniving to sabotage their relationship, and rip them apart. The strangling grip of technology and the seductive pull of social media, testing the depths of their love.

And one night the perverseness of its hold manifested itself while they were making love. Molly had become unusually amorous after dinner, kissing him, and massaging his ego with compliments. "I didn't know spaghetti could be an aphrodisiac," Jarvis had murmured jokingly. Expectations were high, and he had taken Viagra to insure giving one of his command performances. These hot-blooded rendezvous of the past had become insultingly rare, and he wanted to be certain his parts didn't fail.

"Oh God Jarvis."

"I know baby. It's really good tonight," he groaned, attempting to ignore the arthritic ache gripping his hips. *Damn the torpedoes. Full speed ahead.* Watching his wife twist her nipples, and stare wantonly at the ceiling spurred him to rock faster. The room smelled of sex, and he could sense his boys cheering him on. Suddenly the melodious din of Molly's cell intruded upon the squeaking of the bed.

"Oh Jarvis, why now. Can you just hold our place while I get that."

"Hold our place? Are you kidding? Let them leave a message," he puffed.

"Maybe it's important." she said starting to push him away with her feet.

"My God, you're serious!" Jarvis snapped. He frowned, and then lunged forward, thrusting his arm toward the nightstand, and grabbing the phone. He flung it to the carpet. "No more. You need help." He had to duck quickly because his wife was swinging a leg over his head, toward the floor.

"What? I need help? You need help!" she retorted angrily.

"Molly, I love you, but you're addicted to that device. We're making love. Tonight is one for the Guinness Book, sixty and over category, and you want to check your phone?"

"We'll talk about it later," she snapped. "Now look, the tone has stopped, so let me check for any messages." She practically fell out of the bed casting her arm out in a desperate effort to grab her cell.

"No. We'll talk now," he demanded. "We'll talk now, or I'm leaving."

"Leaving? What do you mean? Do you want a divorce? Don't be silly. It's only a phone."

"Exactly," Jarvis returned victoriously. "It's only a phone. I need your full attention sometimes, and this is one of those times. I love you very much. I don't want a divorce. That would be silly. But this is a problem you have. I mean, we're making love!"

"And it's leaving me breathless," Molly hastily agreed, continuing to dart an occasional peek in the direction of the silent cell.

"I was almost there," he said, calmer, but with a hint of annoyance.

"That damn phone," she said with less than believable futility. "I should just give it up."

"Maybe you should. We did great all those years with a landline. And you know what I think about all that social media crap. I wouldn't have any of it if Shelly didn't put pictures of the family online. There's got to be some sort of program which can help you."

Molly didn't say anything, her drawn features exposing the fear and frustration momentarily quieting her resentment. He could almost hear her panicked thinking. "What if he does take it away!? He wouldn't dare!?" She stood up, glancing fretfully at Jarvis, and then at her phone, stepping gingerly over it as she walked quietly out of the bedroom without looking back.

Jarvis remembered the tension. So many years of marriage, and he felt so helpless and awash with despair. It was as if he had been clobbered with the news that she had cancer, and the chances of survival were slim to none. Every time it replayed in his head, the pressure in his chest, and the headache would briefly return. And there would be a wetness on his cheeks. He loved the woman. Didn't she know that?

That night Jarvis tossed and turned as the presence of another dream imposed its will over his desire to sleep. He was hovering within a ceiling of clouds and watching the unfolding scene beneath him of two individuals locked in barely audible conversation. He strained to hear them, but it wasn't until the clouds descended slowly closer that he recognized the faces and the earnest display of candor.

Nice waiting room,' Jarvis scoffed, as if that was important to him. Molly would have said he was wearing his "put on" expression, half disgruntlement, and half reluctant compliance, just like a little boy. *But I need some answers.*

"Mr. Heath, I'm Lauren Welch. I can see you now," a woman announced leaning into the room, and brushing some dangling hair behind her ears.

Pleasant enough smile, Jarvis thought pushing himself up, and following her down the hall. *Looks much too young to help Molly and me. I could be her grandfather.*

I'm glad you came," Lauren said as they sat down in her office.

Jarvis nodded. "Yea, I'm hoping to understand what's going on with my wife, like how can a sixty-four-year-old woman become so consumed by social media, the news, and game apps. She used to love cooking, and baking. Now it's seems everything is ready made from the store and can be shoved in the microwave." He hesitated, hoping the counselor would jump in, but all she did was look at him expectantly.

The sex thing, I don't know if I want to tell her about that episode. Kind of personal. Uh, say something lady. Am I going to do all the talking? Maybe I'm supposed to.

"What prompted your wife to get help?" Lauren finally asked, appearing genuinely concerned.

Jarvis sighed and could feel the rise of cringing self-consciousness enter his face. *Just what I didn't want to discuss,* he thought. "Actually, I was the one who insisted, and she finally agreed. I threatened a divorce. Last week, uh, we were in the bedroom, and, well," he replied, painfully. "Molly's cell went off, and she told me to hold my place." He grimaced as he said it. *This young lady is a professional,* Jarvis reminded himself, as if that would lessen the situation's stigmatizing pain. *Gotta act confident, yet nonchalant.* He pushed the chair back, crossed his legs, and let his shoulders sag. "I told her the phone call could wait, and what we were doing was more important."

Lauren bunched her lips up in a contemplative fashion.

Uh oh, Jarvis thought warily.

"Do you want a divorce?"

"No, of course not! We're soulmates. I said to push her to get help."

"Please don't be offended Mr. Heath, but does Molly enjoy sex?"

"What? Of course!" Jarvis exploded, his eyes cannonade flashes of mutilating disbelief. "What kind of counselor are you?!"

Lauren rocked back in her seat, waving away the hostile response. "This is no reflection on you, Mr. Heath, but if sex is painful, or unfulfilling, it would be easier for your wife to react the way she did," Lauren quickly replied.

Jarvis's growling temperament wilted slightly under what appeared to be a sincere unfurling of sympathy in front of him. "Our love life is great." he said with only a hint of rancor. "Well, it was great" he relented.

"I get that," Lauren replied tenderly. "I don't mean to pry, but any information I get will help us help Molly. Would you agree parts of her life which normally provided satisfaction, have been overshadowed by this compulsion?"

Seems like there's an obvious answer to that question, Jarvis thought, but he answered it anyway. "Yes." He peeked down at the floor, humiliated by his earlier response. "Ah, sorry about the outburst."

Lauren was shaking her head. "It's alright. This must be difficult for you too."

Jarvis sighed again. "I'm baffled. She never, at least overtly, showed any kind of compulsive behavior before this past year, and the incident from the other week. . . and his voice trailed off. "At my wife's age, is it something I've done wrong? Something I should have recognized sooner?" There was an inflection of defeat in his hunt for understanding.

The counselor arched forward as if she was about to share a secret. *Can't fathom what you're thinking girl. Out with it*, Jarvis thought staring back at her.

"It's a disease Mr. Heath. An addiction. One that's become more prevalent in our society, especially over the past five years. It's estimated six to seven percent of Americans have this uncontrollable desire, although it is a global problem. Like excessive gambling, and other addictions, alcohol, drugs, it helps satisfy the insatiable dopaminergic urges that overwhelm some people, and essentially coerces them to spend hours on video games, their cell phones, and all sorts of social media."

"But so late in life?" Jarvis asked.

"It happens," the counselor said, apparently recognizing his consternation with a shake of her head. "Do you have children, Mr. Heath?"

"Yes."

"They're living on their own?"

"Of course. That's the way we raised them."

"Is your wife still working?"

"No."

"So, she has more free time on her hands?"

"I'd say yes."

"Sounds like she's needed something to fill in that void." Lauren shrugged her shoulders and offered him a supplicatory palm. "Social media, the online games are all readily available."

Jarvis shook his head affirmatively, and then peered inquiringly across the desk. "All I want to know is can Molly be helped?"

"I believe she can, if she wants to help herself. It is an addiction and will require her to battle it for the rest of her life. In the beginning there will be a weekly session with me, as well as the three support group meetings, twelve of those each month. Lauren lifted her head slightly and stared across the desk. "Your wife will need your patience and support."

"I know," he answered solemnly. "I needed to hear that she could beat this, or at least control it. Now I have some hope." He stared firmly at Lauren. "I will be her best cheerleader."

CHAPTER FOURTEEN

It had been one of those mornings when little nuisances seemed to have conspired against Jarvis and piled on top of him with their weight of aggravation. First, he discovered the toilet had been running since his two a.m. visit because the chain in the tank needed unsnagging so the stopper would cover the drain hole. Then he was reminded to take the trash to the street just as he heard the garbage truck pulling away from the neighbor's curb. About two hours ago he had stubbed his big toe on the base of the bed as he was stripping the sheets for their monthly wash. Molly had done it weekly, but he figured since there was only him, it wasn't necessary. And now it was early afternoon, the toe still throbbed, and he had foolishly chosen this particular day to waste a few hours getting the Infinity inspected.

"Hate this hard plastic," Jarvis griped as he shimmied around on the seat. "Feels like the screws are pushing into my butt. Probably are, been here so long." He glanced at the other two individuals sharing the waiting area of the garage while their cars were serviced. "I'm just here to get the car inspected," he announced. "Think I will be out of here before the moon comes up?" *No reaction. Not even a disgruntled look to be quiet. Only that blank stare from that woman. Wonder if she's deaf?* The other person was a husky guy in a suit, his attention moored to the laptop balancing on his legs. *Molly liked husky because she said describing someone as over weight or fat was too demeaning. Perhaps I'm dead and they just can't hear me because of the dimensional divide,* Jarvis thought facetiously.

Getting the car inspected is about as American as turkey on Thanksgiving. But rather be chomping on a leg than sitting here. Maybe the government could pay us while we babysit our vehicles.

Jarvis sighed impatiently. *Told the guy behind the desk my daughter is at the hospital about to give birth. That usually speeds things along.* A guilty smile exposed his self-serving intent. He sneaked a peek out the plate glass window. *Yahoo, the Infinity is gone.* Seconds later he heard the familiar beep of the horn.

I'll be out of here before anyone arrives who might know I'm not supposed to be driving. A little paranoid, Jarvis, he taunted. *Think everyone in town knows? And I'll be parked in the driveway prior to the neighbors coming home from work. I think this early afternoon appointment will work out well.*

Jarvis brought a book to read, but he absentmindedly left it on the front seat when he entered the building and now the car was being inspected in one of the bays. "Oh well," he murmured drifting his attention to the television hung on the wall in front of him. "Hmm, a soap opera in the waiting room of a garage? Not very masculine."

Up on the screen, this attractive couple, *as if there were ever any ugly actors on those shows,* was sitting in a restaurant, and it sounded like the man was defending why he had punished her son. "He got me so angry knocking my coffee on the floor. I slapped him on the hand, gently," he quickly added when he saw the mother's face and then I had him sit in the time-out chair. You know I'm trying to work from home and watch him at the same time. It's practically impossible. I think you should pick up more of the load."

Jarvis nodded. Yea, parenting can be quite challenging. *Maybe spouses should be required to get a yearly inspection sticker, and have it glued to one of their shoulders. Let's see, continues to honor and love in sickness and health. Check. Willing to listen, and let the other side win once in a while. Check. Daily hygiene. That was for Molly. She had an issue with adults whose breath or body odor would end a war. Check. Regular parenting skill updates, although most of that was on the job training because each child was different. Check. That's good for starters.* He leaned back and grinned with satisfaction.

A few seconds later Jarvis discovered the man at the restaurant was actually the woman's brother, and he was suggesting that they send their son to childcare. *Wait a minute. Is he the father? There's no other man? Does that mean the brother and sister are the biological parents? Wow. Nothing was off limits on the soaps.* Jarvis shook his head and mumbled, "God, incest. How was that explained to a child actor? He remembered the Flynns in the old neighborhood. I didn't find out the meaning of the word until I was thirteen. I must have been slow or should have been watching soap operas."

The voices on the TV faded into the background as Jarvis willingly submitted to a beckoning reminiscence of him and Molly sitting on the shoreline at Indian Lake six years ago. It was an idyllic location to spend a romantic moment with his wife while waddling ducks patrolled the grassy edges and the occasional telltale sign of fish broke the surface, leaving ringlets of water in their wake. Across the lake stretched a sparkling reflection of the setting sun as it brushed the water with broad strokes of ruddy complexion.

"Beautiful isn't it. So serene," Jarvis said pouring each of them another glass of cabernet and setting them down on the grass.

"I like beautiful and serene," Molly replied resting her head on his shoulder.

"I wouldn't have appreciated this when I was younger."

"You had too much going on. School. Flying jets. Women."

Jarvis felt a teasing elbow nudge his chest as he gave her a sideway glance. "Think you're so smart, huh, lady. But all that seems so long ago," he said wistfully.

"And now here we are," Molly said. "So many wonderful memories later." A peaceful silence wrapped around them, infrequently being interrupted by the brazen bellow of a love-struck frog announcing its presence.

"What are you thinking about?" Jarvis quietly asked after a few minutes went by.

"The past twelve months," his wife replied. "So much has changed for me, for you. The three weekly meetings, the one with the counselor, and the two with ITAA."

"Uh, Internet and Technology Addiction Anonymous."

"You finally got it right," Molly said with a half-smile. "Who would have guessed there would be a need for such an organization. We have six in the group now. I'm the oldest."

"Really?"

"Mm, guess I don't talk much about it. We try to keep things just between us."

"I know I've said this before Molly, but it must be difficult being surrounded by social media and video games." There was a tenor of inquisitive concern in his voice.

"The very reason the meetings are so important. We can talk about the temptations and provide support for each other. Getting the phone with the online access blocked was a good idea." Molly stopped, her face briefly lost in a cloud of private contemplation. "The younger people really struggle with the addiction. It's ruined some relationships. I'm glad you urged me to get into the program."

Jarvis shrugged. "You had to make the decision to get help."

"One of the best decisions I ever made." She paused and kissed Jarvis on the cheek. "Thank you for not looking over my shoulder. You trust me and that's very important."

"Trust is very important." Jarvis said, momentarily frowning at the indiscretion from his past that flicked in and out of his head.

"Is my big, strong man alright," Molly asked looking up at him.

"Yea, he's okay. Just very happy to be here with his wife."

CHAPTER FIFTEEN

It was the steady pelting of angry rain upon the roof, and the insistent rapping of drops against the windows that woke Jarvis up, "Great way to start the day," he grumbled, shaking his fists in exaggerated disgust. "I planned to mow the lawn and begin painting the house." The latter project a draconian ordeal which he had postponed for weeks because it required scraping off the peeling slivers of white exterior, sanding, and then brushing on the new coat of paint. *Besides, the house doesn't look bad from the street. It can wait a few more weeks. That's a valid excuse*, his procrastinating side reasoned.

Jarvis's aching joints conspired to keep him in bed even as he inched his way over to the side. "Rather stay right where I am," he complained mercifully. But then dolefully thought, *"The day I don't move, one hour will become twenty-four, then forty-eight. Won't ever feel like throwing the blanket off again. Swim in my own pee. The body will wither. I'll be called Twiggy at my Memorial service.*

Hmm, shave, eat breakfast. I can do that. Maybe the rain will let up soon," he thought audaciously, despite the persistent patter, and gray light peeping into the room as he parted the curtains.

However, the storm continued its insurgent march through the neighborhood into the afternoon, bringing with it the yawning monotony that strafed Jarvis with impatience. He turned on the television, but the tedium of the talk shows and soaps only exacerbated the relentless emptiness. So instead, he picked up the spy novel from the night before, ignoring Anna Karenina, still waiting patiently on the shelf for the touch of his hands. An hour passed before Jarvis looked out the windows again, and glowered at the high, wet grass, and the pooling of water in the areas that were brown and muddy. "Hmm, maybe I should try sodding those," he muttered, sliding a restive hand over his head. "Enough rain already!"

His eyes hurt from reading so much, and the sad part was, several chapters in, he remembered finishing the book six months before. "*Days like this dull the senses,*" he reassured himself. "*I'm not losing it, yet.*" He forced himself to close his eyes, and soon a reminiscent reel of pubescent musing distanced him from the wearisome weather outside.

"*Life is an everchanging collage of perspectives.*" It was an axiom he had read at the bottom of some magazine many years before and stuck because of its relevance to his own life. What might have been acceptable behavior when he was younger, Jarvis now looked upon as reckless and youthful indiscretion, like the time he ran through the college campus with a herd of other exuberantly drunk males. Well, not running exactly, more like lunging, staggering and jostling. When they got to the female dorms, they would drop their shorts and moon the buildings to the cheers and lighthearted screams of the women inside. Jarvis never reckoned he could be suspended or expelled for such behavior until two members of the security force arrived at one of the residences in their squad car. "Shit. This isn't going to look good on my resume."

But when two female officers emerged from the vehicle, the group of fifteen or so, grinned at each, turned around, and dropped their shorts again. Jarvis managed to peek over his shoulder in time to see the women shaking their heads in apparent bemusement, and then drive away three minutes later to yells of perceived almightiness.

However the axiom could not have been more appropriate than when he was 12 and first noticed the bristly growth of hair under his arms. He was practically jubilant as he prodded them with his fingers.

"About time," Jarvis declared, a little louder than he intended.

"Huh?" his father said coming into the bathroom.

"Nothing," he replied with some embarrassment. Glimpsing over at his dad, and then back into the mirror, he quickly slid a hand around his chin while the old man was peeing in the toilet. "*Yep, four or five prickly hairs there too. Be shaving before long. Two men using the bathroom now.*"

Peeking over at his father again, he suddenly felt as if a blindfold had been removed from his eyes. Just minutes before the old man was still the giant who could build rock walls, down beers while watching football with his overexcited friends, and disappear every weekday morning to reappear magically at night. And when he was a kid, his father was the only one who could momentarily steal away his mother's attention, and then give it back to him when they were done clinging to each other and kissing. "Funny how I can remember stuff like that." Jarvis remarked.

He remembered looking over at his father and seeing a man who seemed to have shrunk in height, had thin, veiny, arms, and scraggily, gray hair. "Brain working overtime, and wearing out the roots," he could hear his dad saying.

Yet despite this flash of sobering epiphany, he was still the one Jarvis listened to when he needed help correcting his batting stance and swing in Little League. And the parent to whom he guiltily confessed stealing a football from his cousin because his was lost, and who firmly encouraged him to return it with an apology. His father also showed him how to cast his fishing line into the lake, and not into somebody's arm like his friend Billy had done. That was so long ago.

Jarvis had his turn filling those shoes when Michael and Sherry probably looked askance at him at some point and wondered what happened to their to father. Where did the old man go who used to throw them up in the air when they were in the pool together, or who helped them late at night with procrastinated school projects, or who muttered too often about the perceived lack of common sense in the people he saw around him. Now, even that seemed so long ago.

It must have been the sudden silencing of the rain's staccato drumming that gave Jarvis a start, or maybe it was being accosted by the gurgling in his stomach.

"*Something's wrong. Oh, the rain stopped,*" he thought. "*Getting hungry too. Maybe have those leftovers from yesterday. The kids never liked them. More for me.*" He laced his fingers together and cupped the back of his head. A wry smile crept between his lips as reminiscent swigs of quixotic reflection coaxed him to murmur, "Plenty of times they got to see their old man in action, and sometimes looking like an idiot. Made me human, and not an ogre. Molly would say she was the only adult in the house. Pretty funny."

Jarvis's memory of Shelly's eighth grade English project momentarily pushed aside the urge to eat, which for him was pretty amazing since eating had become a treasured function of every day. But the story about their encounter with the deer was in an archive of memories he would never forget.

How did she start it? Oh yeah, I remember. "What would you think of a man who would drive off the road and get stuck in a farm field just to avoid hitting some deer. Well, that man is my father."

Both kids had been in the back seat after a day spent at the Air and Space Museum in Dulles, and a lunch at their favorite fast food. Molly had been sick, and declined to go. They were almost home when the doe and her fawns pranced onto the road, and stopped there, apparently oblivious of any impending doom as they stared Jarvis down.

Michael was shouting, "Stupid deer. Stupid deer."

Shelly screamed, "Don't hit them dad. Don't hit them."

The pavement was wet from a recent storm, and there were farms on either side, the left one with an embankment running alongside the road. Jarvis braked, and yanking the steering wheel to the right, skidded into a field of hay, the muddy ground helping the automobile jerk to a stop. About thirty seconds later, the deer walked nonchalantly past, just giving them a brief, "Pardon me" look.

"Oh, how beautiful," Shelly said.

"Wonder what venison tastes like," Michael asked.

"Glad everyone is okay. Wonder how we're going to get out of here?" Jarvis had muttered quietly, as the wheels spun beneath them.

He called 911, and reported their dilemma, and soon a local cop pulled up on the road.

"Neat," Michael said

"Daddy, are you going to jail?"

"No, I am not going to jail. Just going to get some help to pull us out of here." He got out of the car and waited for the approaching officer.

"Decided to plow the field with my car instead of the tractor," he joked, and then, *"Takes his job real seriously,"* when there was no hint of humor on the other man's face.

"What's the problem?"

"Is he kidding me?" Jarvis thought. "Uh, three deer jumped in front of the car, and the safest way to avoid them was steering over here. The kids in the back are fine."

"The road is wet mister. How fast were you going?"

"Forty-five? Fifty?"

"Too fast for the conditions of the road. If you had been going slower, you could have safely stopped. I'll have to give you a ticket for driving recklessly, then call a truck to tow you out. License. Registration please."

"But officer, how was I to know," Jarvis started until images of lights and bells at a railroad crossing abruptly flashed into his head. "Sure, I'll get them," twisting around, and leaning back into the car.

"Dad, are you going to jail?" Michael asked.

"Daddy, are we going to jail?" a pale, tearful Shelly asked.

Jarvis responded with an exasperated sigh. "No one's going anywhere. The policeman is just doing his job. He's going to call someone to pull us out. I will call your mother and she can come pick you up."

"Is he going to put cuffs on you?"

"If you don't be quiet Michael, I will have him put handcuffs on you."

"Would you really?" his son asked hesitantly. There was a squeak in his voice.

"If you don't be quiet, you'll find out."

Shelly began to cry. "I don't like him sometimes, but I wouldn't want my brother to go to jail."

"I'm waiting sir," the officer announced loudly.

"Be right there. My son and daughter are upset."

The sudden creak of the recliner, and the obstinate return of his hunger pried Jarvis from his revery. "Thank God Molly was feeling well enough to pick up the kids while I had the car pulled out." he uttered gratefully. He snorted. *The whole incident is kind of funny now, but then, it absolutely was not.* He shrugged the tightness out of his shoulders and neck. "Well, think I'll heat up the leftovers," and pushed himself out of the chair.

CHAPTER SIXTEEN

"Going a little fast, aren't you?" Jarvis asked, more of an admonishment than a question. He was leaning toward Michael and peeking at the speedometer. "Want to finish me off early?"

"Uh, no dad. I'm in the car with you, and I don't have any death wish, yet," he said glancing at his father. "Although, you have been known to push people to their limit. So, watch it old man," he jested. "Besides, we're only going five miles above the speed limit."

"Yea, right," Jarvis grumped, not masking his disapproval. "That's not how I taught you to drive. Nice and easy in the parking lot."

"Yea, right," Michael mimicked. "You left out it was a manual, and after the parking lot, you drove us to the top of Benson street, the steepest one in town, put on the emergency brake, glanced over at me as you got out, and announced, "Your turn to drive." You knew we still had to get over the crest of the hill. My palms were so wet with apprehension, I thought they would slip off the steering wheel because you expected me to coordinate the pedals, so we wouldn't roll into the vehicle behind us."

"You learned to balance the clutch and gas didn't you."

Michael responded to his father's sanctimony with a dubious grin, which Jarvis interpreted as an admission he was right.

Knew he'd appreciate what I did for him, Jarvis thought confidently. For the next few minutes, silence filled the automobile, and he just stared out the window. *Doctor visit went well enough. Blood pressure good. Lungs clear. Heart still able to crank out the blood. Guess I'll be living long enough to help him pay off the vacation home in the Bahamas.*

A quick smirk abruptly disappeared beneath a roll of melancholic reminiscence. *Molly always liked this ride through the valley. Fully dressed trees crowding the road like they were pushing and shoving to get across. She did have a way with words.*

Jarvis's eyes misted. After the medical appointment, he and Michael stopped by her grave. Molly loved yellow roses and they had put some in the bronze vase by the headstone, then tidied up the grass around the site. Afterward, his son had given him twenty minutes alone with her while he went to get the truck washed.

"You alright, dad?" Michael intrusively asked, his voice colored with deliberate concern. Jarvis could sense his prying eyes.

"Yes. Just thinking. Wondering why your mother and I decided to be buried when we already had made the decision to be cremated. The cemetery has a columbarium. Fancy word, huh? It's like a hotel for urns, without the checkout."

Michael dropped a hint of a smile. "When you and mom asked Shelly and me to decide where your remains should go, which was kind of sick if you ask me, you complained it wouldn't give you enough elbow room. Mom finally relented. That's why you bought that little piece of Real Estate you can call your own.

"Oh, that's right. Need my elbow room."

"And I replied that you'll be dead, actually, ashes, so what difference does it make? Then you said that since I had never been dead, how could I possibly know.

"That's right.," Jarvis agreed. "Course then you mentioned I had never been dead either. Touche."

Michael nodded.

Jarvis let the passing scenery briefly grab his attention before speaking again. "Your mother was a very good woman. I got lucky."

"The best, dad."

"Mm," Jarvis murmured, caught up in an eddy of heartfelt contemplation. "You think the trip to Heaven is painless? I know that's where she's at."

"More than likely," Michael answered, courting his father's attention with a questioning veneer.

"What's that look for," Jarvis asked.

"Surprised, that's all. Been two years since mom passed, and you're wondering about her trip to Heaven. And when I was younger, you weren't particularly keen on all this God stuff. Christmas and Easter were the exceptions. Had to become religious on those days."

"Well, I got older and wiser," Jarvis answered. "Always been quiet about certain beliefs." He wrinkled his forehead and stared reflectively out the windshield before returning to the conversation. "I still have many questions without answers, but when I noticed how often the number seven seemed to crop up in the scriptures, I figured that was a sign. I began to think there might be some truth to the Bible. For example, seven days for creation, resting on the seventh one. Seven days in our week. Seven years of good harvest and seven years of famine according to Joseph. Seven trips around Jericho before it fell. Seven miles per second to break free of earth's gravity."

"I don't know what one has to do with the other, but wow! When did you become an expert, and really?" Michael asked with astonishment. "Seven miles per second? That fast?"

"Something I still remember from my aviator days," his father admitted. "Anyhow, the thing about the sevens, just some trivia I picked up along the way. Maybe a connection somewhere."

"Hmm, interesting," Michael said ponderously. Then, "You know dad, you surprise me sometimes."

"Surprise myself. I'll take that as a compliment."

"You and mom liked to dance. I bet she's waiting up there for you to lead her across the floor."

"Would be disappointed if she wasn't," Jarvis answered, still feeling diminished by the morning's somber visit. "However, my best moves are when I step on dog shit and do a little jig. Amazing how light on your feet one can become."

Michael chuckled, and then let his father continue.

"And trying to wipe it off the soles of your shoes. Disgusting."

As they sat in silence again, Jarvis's thoughts traveled back to his wife, and the last few years she spent battling the addiction to her phone, internet, and social media. It still surprised him that Molly had gotten so caught up in the milieu, and let it rule her day. Particularly at her age. *After sixty, no more baggage. That's the rule. She laid that one to rest* He grimaced at the unintended pun.

She claims to have over two thousand "Friends" on her Facebook page, he had explained to the kids after Molly started her outpatient sessions. A*nd was constantly playing video games. It's no wonder your mother spent so much of her time online. She would watch CNN, Fox, and other news programs throughout the day too. For different viewpoints?* Jarvis had shaken his head in bafflement then, and now, in sentimental acceptance. *The whole situation* *disrupted our lives. It's not exactly how I expected we would spend retirement, but the truth is, I love her,* finishing with a hint of vulnerability, an emotion he would excuse as a lapse of self-control.

Jarvis's thoughts hitched a ride on the song playing on the radio, and he murmured along with lyrics that spoke about starting over. Exactly what he and Molly had done once she admitted there was a problem and immersed herself confronting the enemy which tempted her every day. After she died, he had to carry on again, alone this time, and make a life for himself.

A sudden ka-thump jolted Jarvis from his reverie. "Do you purposely hit every pothole in the road?" he asked.

"Only when you're in the car, dad. Want to make sure you're still alive."

"Funny," Jarvis replied, noting on the GPS screen they were an hour away from the house. *Think I'll eat, watch some TV, and go to bed early when I get home. Been a long day. Maybe get a little shuteye now, if Michael will turn down the radio, and* not talk. *Maybe drive on the smooth side of the highway.*

The grave was on a grassy knoll that overlooked the whole cemetery. There was a towering oak that stood guard nearby, and its tentacled branches provided Molly with afternoon shade and coolness

Michael had opened a beach chair for his father and promised to pick him up after the truck was cleaned. "Hope I don't forget." he jested.

"No problem. Take you out of the will." Jarvis threatened facetiously. He watched Michael walk away, and then slowly drifted his attention back to the plot in front of him. His lips pressed grimly, and his eyes watered. "Feel like I'm on a first date, and don't know where to start," he murmured. "Molly, you still have that effect on me. My heart beats faster, and I get tongue tied. That's why I wrote down a few things, just in case my brain stops working.

"Uh, sorry about not visiting you regularly. Poor excuse, but the months just seem to skip by. Someday though, it'll be my turn, and my name will fill in that empty space beneath yours. Then I can haunt the kids for not visiting more often."

Jarvis surveyed the area. "Beautiful day. You must have known I was coming. Arranged it with the Big Guy. Think you could put in a good word for me?"

Sighing, he backed his butt against the chair, and reached into his shirt pocket for the list. "Told you I jotted down some thoughts. Hmm, top of the list, bananas. Attempt to eat three or four a week, but they brown up so quickly. Maybe eat all of them at a single meal and get all my potassium at one time."

A vexing regret momentarily clouded his face until a soulful recollection lifted it away. "Miss you so much. Your sleepy scent in the morning when I would wrap my arms around you for a kiss and hug. Then you would practically scold me, "I just got out of bed. My breath must smell terrible." Honestly, it sometimes did, but I didn't care. Mine probably smelled bad every morning. And of course, a photo of you is still propped against the pillow on your side of the bed. I say good-night to it, and good-morning. I suspect some people might have me committed.

Guess who dropped in to see me. Your brother Ken. Haven't seen him in quite a while. Sally passed earlier this year. He's bent over. Bald. But otherwise seems in good spirits.

Weird. The past six, seven months been dreaming a lot, mostly about all the fun we had together. Reaffirms how fortunate I was to have you in my life. I will always love you Molly." He paused before continuing.

"So proud of the way you faithfully attended those weekly meetings. You said you were doing it for us as well as yourself. That meant everything to me. It took a lot of courage and fortitude."

Jarvis peeked over his shoulders. "Don't need anyone observing me talking into thin air. They wouldn't understand. The Infinity still runs well. The kids think they took my car keys away. However, I had an extra set made just in case. All I do is go to the store and deliver the meals. Glad they don't check the mileage."

Trying to take care of myself. A little bleeding from the back end, so I had a colonoscopy done. Going to be the highlight of my year. Probably why I fart all the time. The doc says all they found were hemorrhoids.

Michael and Shelly are doing well. He's got a new girlfriend who doesn't like to cook. See how long that lasts with his appetite. The grandkids are enthralled with all the new technology. Despite that, they seem well adjusted and happy." Jarvis paused, and then, "I'm going to be quiet now, and just enjoy this time together."

Resting his monologue, he closed his eyes, and listened to the twittering birds, a riding mower in the distance, and luxuriated in the swathe of peace that descended upon him.

CHAPTER SEVENTEEN

If there were standards men used to judge their successes, and failures in life, Jarvis had little doubt that his own was a compendium of blessings. His most humbling achievement being the woman lying beside him for thirty-nine years. Every morning when he rolled over and laid his eyes on Molly, he realized she was the best gift he had ever received. Luck had truly smiled upon him. Even through the darkest hours of their marriage love and respect had kept them together.. This was the message he hoped his grandson would retain from the interview they were having for Billy's English assignment., "The Most Outstanding Person I Know." *Quite an accolade*, Jarvis thought with bemusement. *Although if he knew some famous athlete or musician, pretty sure I'd rank a little lower on the totem pole. I'm the best that he's got. I hope my responses don't blow holes in the whole perception of me being special.* They had spent much of the time sitting on the front porch, sipping lemonade between bouts of questions and answers.

"Ya know Billy," he said, "Sure you want to continue this conversation? Have to say, I'm pretty much an ordinary guy. Not a politician or president of a company. Never had to save someone's life, thank God. Push on the chest, push on the chest, that's all I know. Never any reason for my name to be in the paper or on the evening news. And when the internet came along decades later, no mention of my name on Twitter, or on any of that other techno crap. Excuse me. Don't tell your mother," Jarvis whispered leaning forward. His grandson just grinned, as if the words techno crap weren't offensive and worthy to write in his article.

"Even my stint as a Navy pilot wasn't meant to impress anyone. Well, maybe my father, your great grandfather. And yea, I believed I owed the country something, and still believe we all do, but back then, it was mostly about being selfish, and learning how to fly jets."

"That sounds exciting.'

"I thought so." Jarvis answered.

"Wasn't it dangerous?"

"Every time I stepped into the cockpit. You just shoved the thought to the back of your mind."

"Did you shoot down any enemy planes?"

Jarvis chuckled. "I flew in Vietnam. It was more bombing runs than aerial combat."

"Oh?" Billy responded with a questioning lilt. "What does that mean?"

"I had to," and Jarvis stopped mid-sentence, *How do I clean this up? I don't want to tell him I killed innocent women and children when I targeted the Vietcong.* "I had to attack the enemy on the ground. Make it a little safer for our soldiers."

"Oh. Make it a little easier for them, huh?"

"A little," Jarvis replied, a pensive smile trenched between his lips. He watched his grandson scribbling furiously to get it down.

"You sold houses after you flew jets. How come you quit flying?"

"Neck injury. Notice, I can't turn my head completely from one side to the other."

"Oh, too bad." Billy murmured.

Hope he isn't getting bored. Jarvis thought uncertainly. *Didn't think I would put him to sleep.*

"What do you find important Pops?"

"Hmm, easy one," Jarvis said shifting his weight on the sofa. "Loving my family. I was blessed with the best.." His eyes glazed over in reminiscence. *Especially Molly. She gave life a certain flair.* A hand tapping his knee lured him back."

"What? Oh yea," He shrugged his shoulders unashamedly. "Also love of country, and the two Rs, responsibility and respectfulness. You can add honesty and fairness to that list too. Those values and traits helped me get through life."

"Sounds like a lot to live up to?"

"Comes naturally being brought up in a military family. Your great grandfather spent twenty years in the service."

"Wow, that's a long time. I haven't been in school that long." He appeared to mull that around before starting to speak again. "What do you think is good about living in the new millennium?"

"Being alive, and able to talk with my grandson."

"Ha, you're very funny Pops."

"It's true, but how about making new memories."

"That'll do. So, what do you think is bad about the new millennium?"

"The techno crap," they both echoed.

Billy shook his head with a snort of amusement. "Thought you'd say that. Do you have any last comments?"

"How about this? There's still hope for the younger generation."

That was the end of the interview, but an hour later, after a peanut butter and jelly sandwich, Jarvis was back outside, slumped in a favorite, white rattan rocker. His chin bobbed against his chest with every second or third snorty breath as he unconsciously basked in a conversation with Molly, shortly before she got appendicitis, and was admitted into the hospital.

It was a peaceful, autumn afternoon, and they were on the porch, caught up in playful bandying of past stories and pithy observations they had forged over the years. The season had become Molly's favorite time of year, with its lustful display of flirty colored leaves, and hints of the coolness which was to come.

"Do you remember the first time I walked in on you?"

Molly tilted her head to the side and eyed him like the last few marbles had finally rolled out of his head. "Good way to continue a conversation," she said lightly laughing. "And just like you. Yes, I was on the toilet at the time. I didn't know whether to throw the box of Kleenex at you, or scream, "I'm going to the bathroom!"

"You did both," Jarvis reminded her. "The corner of that box hurt."

"Poor baby," Molly said with no contrition.

"Always knocked after that."

"You actually grew a few brain cells." She couldn't suppress a smirk from her face. "You piloted jets in the Navy, yet you're like a little boy sometimes."

Jarvis responded with his "aw shucks," expression, and then, "They're pretty good, huh? Haven't missed a beat."

Molly followed his gaze to the street. "Been a while since I've seen anyone jumping rope. I think our Shelly was the last one."

"And she was good," Jarvis said. He glanced over at his wife. "Bet you were good in your day."

"Jumping rope? I can't remember back that far." she replied with an air of teasing devilry.

"Yea, likely. The other day, you mentioned writing a story when you were nine about a stray cat looking for someone to love, and a week later your mother brought one home."

"A subtle hint." Molly said splaying out her hands in tacit innocence. "I loved Pony. I'll never forget her."

"Pony? You didn't tell me her name... for a cat?"

Molly giggled. "I really wanted a horse or a pony, but I knew there was no way my parents would get one for me."

"And that's why we're still together after all these years," Jarvis wittily declared. "You're as crazy as I am." He paused, and reaching out, cupped her hand in his. "Hope you're feeling the warmth."

"Oh baby, I've been feeling it ever since I heard the words I love you thirty-eight years ago." She hesitated for a moment as Jarvis chuckled, and then peered at him with a mischievous expression, her eyes becoming big and black. "I never told you this, but one of the reasons I married you was because of the way you eat."

"Huh?"

Molly tittered again. "My mother said if a man chews with his mouth closed, grab him. He's a good one and don't let him get away."

"Really? She said that?" Jarvis asked with an unconstrained guffaw.

"She honestly did. But I don't know what she would have said about some of your other habits."

"You mean I have habits that annoy you?"

"Do you want a list of them now or later?"

Jarvis looked over at his wife and grinned. "Ooh baby, you're hot today, and I love it"

"What can I say, life is really good for two sentimental old fools," and she gave his fingers a loving squeeze.

Chapter Eighteen

"I know that voice," Jarvis mumbled as he opened his eyes and groped through the haziness in his head. "Shelly?"

"Finally awake, huh." She squeezed his hand. "You've been snoozing for a while dad."

He tried to shrug his shoulders, but the right one gripped him in a vice, and awakened the pain his somnolence had temporarily disguised.

"God, what did I do?" Jarvis grunted. He squiggled back against the bed, and abruptly knifing pain plunged into his backside, and between his legs. "Damn, what's wrong with my ass. . .uh, butt?

Shelly's humored smile transiently awarded her father's chivalrous effort not to swear, as if that was something new.

"The doctor said you have a minor crack in your pelvis, and you dislocated your right shoulder. He had to put it back in place."

"A minor crack in my pelvis? I think the doctor has a minor crack in his head," Jarvis exclaimed. "It's worse than the day I disturbed all those hornets, and I ran around the yard stripping my clothes off."

His daughter giggled. "I remember that day. Mom was yelling, "Not your shorts. Not your shorts."

Jarvis harrumphed, and even that caused him to groan. "And this thing," he griped, pulling on his IV line. "Think they could at least shave some of the hair off before applying this duct tape!"

"Now dad, they don't use duct tape. But you do seem uncomfortable. Let me check if you can have more pain medicine."

"No. I'll be alright," he growled, putting his left hand up defensively despite the semblance of grimacing discomfort on his face. *I can do this*, he thought. Shelly was just rolling her eyes.

"The hospital is going to keep you for a few days to do a few tests, and then send you to a nursing home for some therapy."

Jarvis pulled back and narrowed his eyes disapprovingly. "I don't need any nursing home! I can have therapy at the house."

"Dad, stop being a tough guy. We'll discuss it later," his daughter said firmly. She moved around to confront Jarvis directly. "Daddy, that S on your chest wore off a long time ago. What were you doing on the ladder?"

"I had to clean the gutters."

"Michael said he would do that."

"Some things can't wait."

"You're stubborn." She shook her head reprovingly, and then abruptly grinned at him. "You look so guilty."

"Well, I'm not," Jarvis uttered with annoyance. "The ladder slid, and I fell into the bushes. A few scratches and bruises, and my shoulder hurts. And now my ass."

"Shelly smirked." You're lucky you didn't hit your head or break a hip."

"The bushes cushioned my fall."

"Thankfully."

"About the nursing home."

"Daddy!" she reprimanded gently. "Contrary to what you think, you're not getting younger."

"My father was eighty-four, and he still talked about those older people."

"We're not talking about your father, dad. Now stop being so ornery, and let the nurses and doctors take care of you." A scolding love, with a benign slap upon the old man's bulging ego.

Jarvis rebutted Shelly with a disgruntled stare. "You can't force me into a nursing home!"

"Daddy, I love you. I want you to be safe."

"Oh, sling the love crap somewhere else," he said trying to sound angry.

His daughter smiled dismissively. "Mom was right. You act tough, but you're just mush inside."

"Well, you're both wrong." he bellowed, shaking his head obstinately at the patronizing volley. He turned his head, and glared at the wall, not caring whether Shelly heard the next eviscerating comment or not. "Damn women."

Thirty minutes later, Shelly left for the day, and Jarvis was alone. He felt his strength returning, what little he apparently had left at his age, and his thinking was more ordered, and incisive. "Hmm, let me check this place out," he muttered. "Not as scary as Molly's room even though I'm the patient now." He glanced to his left. "Window to the parking lot I see. None in Molly's."

In those last few weeks, the doctors and nurses had done everything they could to keep his wife alive. Her ICU room was cluttered with IV lines, wires, tubes, a ventilator, and bags of medicine. It was never serene, even if the medical staff weren't in the room, because there were always ticking pumps, and beeping monitors. For days after her passing, he woke up in sweats, believing he was the one hooked up to all the intrusive equipment. He would have preferred it that way.

Jarvis checked his forearm again and groaned as he felt the IV pulling on more hairs. "Ya come in for a cold, and they stick one of these things in your arm. What a nuisance." This time he moved his arm slowly when he reached for a cup of water and took a sip. "No wonder people lose weight in a hospital. They make it impossible to feed yourself."

He winced trying to shuffle his butt to the right. "Uh, this damn ass of mine, and everywhere else when I try to move. Oh! What's that pain," he yelped, and looked underneath the sheet. "God, a hose shoved in Fred. This place is a regular torture chamber." He tugged on the tube to see if it would allow more leeway to shift his weight. "Damn! Feels like I'm pulling my bladder out! Wonder where else I've got one? Where's that alarm button? I need some medicine."

Shortly after the nurse administered something for pain, the discomfort began to recede, and Jarvis felt more relaxed. "Ah. . . this is more like it." He nestled his head on the pillow as scenes with Molly swarmed into his head. All of them good. Birthdays. Holidays. Vacations. Even the first time they met. He teasingly called it their unexpected first date. She always disagreed, calling it just one big embarrassment.

She had been backing out of her driveway in a neighborhood where he was showing a house, and he didn't have time to brake or swerve. "Backed out right in front of me," he'd recite to anyone who asked, and then with a sentimental glint in his eyes, "Glad she did it. Funny thing though, she was working for an insurance agency back then, and was leaving her house to check the damage on a client's automobile." But that was as far as the story would go. He never mentioned how humiliated, and apologetic his wife had been. Although the timing could not have been better because Jarvis swore it was love at first sight. For him, anyway.

"Hardly any damage," he had said trying to console her. "Perhaps we don't need to contact our insurance companies."

"Really?" she said with a nervous gasp of relief. She laid her open hands across her diaphragm to still her anxious breaths and allow herself to speak. "It's ironic," she replied, apparently more composed. "I work for one. Let me call my client and tell him I'll be a little late. Got into an accident." Molly practically choked on the words as she turned and walked back to the house. No cell phones in those days.

Nice butt, Jarvis noted. *Wonder if she would go out with me? Maybe lay a little guilt trip on her.*

Lingering pain breached the wall of his reminiscence and reminded Jarvis where he was. But his eyes still glint with mischievous satisfaction remembering that first encounter. "First time I rear ended a woman and didn't know her name." He peered sheepishly upward. "Sorry Babe. Couldn't resist. But I love you very much," he added in case a simple, "I'm sorry," wasn't enough.

Jarvis's thoughts were hijacked by images of Molly's last visit to the hospital. *Who could have guessed she would never leave.*

A relatively simple and safe procedure, the surgeon had said. Jarvis felt reassured because the same operation had been performed when his own appendix was removed. She was healthier than him. What could go wrong?

Probably back in high school he had learned there were bacteria on the skin, and ones residing in the body. He never figured any of them would mount an attack against his beautiful Molly and spread like the root system of the weeds she always complained about. Fifteen, insufferable days of antibiotics, intravenous heart drugs, and medicine to stabilize her blood pressure.

At the end, Michael and Shelly had been at the bedside with him. Holding his wife's still warm hand, he gave it sporadic squeezes, encouraging her to pull a fast one, and startle them all with a miracle. But that didn't happen.

"Molly, we had a great life. We have great kids. I'll be alright. I love you."

Those were his last words to her.

The first six months had been tough, no doubt about it. Memories seized Jarvis's stoic façade, wrenching tears from his eyes, and testing his reserve of strength. It was a losing battle until he decided to partition off that part of his life and move forward with a new one. He could never forget her, and kept plenty of photos around the house, but he wouldn't allow the patented scent of her presence hold him back. He would celebrate what they had together, but he would not be held captive by it.

He had been privileged being married to the best wife in the world, and during the past two years, had become quite settled in his ways. Jarvis feared another woman would only disrupt the peaceful rhythm of each day, and some, might mistakenly try to forge a new man for themselves. "Not this one," he vowed. "And no nursing home!" he growled as a reminder.

Chapter Nineteen

"I swear, I'll be kicking and screaming before they drag me into a Nursing Home, or some Assisted Living." Jarvis said with impassioned resolve to his chuckling gym buddies. That had been five years ago, when he was still pretending to work out with the other old guys and using the time more to socialize than sweat off pounds. But the incentive to be there even for the camaraderie waned with Molly's passing. *We're just a bunch of paunchy men with skinny arms and legs. Who am I kidding. We won't solve the world's problems or even the ones in our own lives.* A phony excuse to justify his absence from the gym. *Someday, maybe I'll return*, he had thought halfheartedly, but that day never did arrive.

Anyhow, Jarvis thought it was ironic that his sworn objection to ever being incarcerated (his word), in a place like Great Expectations taunted him while he sat on the throne in his private room. He had been admitted two days earlier after begrudgingly conceding to Shelly's efforts to get him into the rehab. But he still felt a sense of betrayal when neither of the kids would entertain the idea of him going home for his therapy.

"Great Expectations. What kind of name is that anyway? It just gives a pretense of false hope and steals your damn dignity." Jarvis harrumphed. 'The only expectation most people have coming here is that instead of walking out, they'll be leaving on a stretcher staring up at the ceiling I don't care how nice it is, I'm going to get the hell out of here before the Grim Reaper says, "Your turn mister."

He did a grimaced shift of his butt, moving about three inches on the seat, and then sank down on his right cheek. He crooked his neck to the left so he could see the framed photograph of his wife on the dresser through the doorway. "Molly, I hope you're not offended, but I'm not ready to leave yet. I just want to spend a little more time with the kids, and grandkids so I have something more to tell you when I get up there."

Right now, he also wanted his shoulder and pelvis to heal so he could make a blurred exit out the front door. With the right arm splinted close to his chest, it was not easy to do even simple tasks.

"This getting old business sucks," Jarvis muttered as he waited impatiently on the toilet for a nurse to come and wipe his butt. He yanked on the red emergency cord again, as if that would bring help sooner. "I could have fallen and cracked my head open, but they're probably busy on their cellphones!"

He sighed resignedly, and then, stirring up his anger, "Damn, I hate being dependent on somebody else!" And then reassuringly, "At least this is temporary. I'm better off than a lot of people my age. Still living on my own, still can carry on a coherent conversation and cook pretty good, too." Usually, he could rationalize himself out of these funky trespasses into self-pity.

Just can't reach my back side anymore, he griped silently. 'Damn rotator cuff. The doc said it was partially torn from the fall. You'll have to use your other hand. Idiot. Thinks I'm ambidextrous. So humiliating." He pressed his lips together in unrepentant disgust.

Abruptly Jarvis wrinkled his nose and snorted with a telltale "ugh" as the putrid stench of soiled underwear swirled around him. "Ten seconds sooner and everything would have been in the bowl. No heart problem. No brain problem. Just problems when I must take a dump. Shit."

Now it had become a race to see if he could get to the bathroom in time. "A freaking countdown," he grumped to one of the residents he just met. The man was propped up in a chair, and kept uttering "food, food", whenever someone passed. "From the moment the urge first hits, I have one minute to find a seat to plop my skinny ass. Course I hobble around like a gimpy horse because my damn ass is broken. But so far, this is my first accident. It did help memorizing the locations of all the restrooms on the first and second floors from a map they gave me when I first came in here. Shows where all the fire exits are too. Guess they expect the place to burn down?"

Three doors down, Harry Turkle had offered his own bathroom. Just had to knock four times and shout his name, but the guy shuffled worse than Jarvis hobbled, and always had the television blaring. It would be a disaster if his was the only bathroom.

Jarvis grunted as he attempted to change his position, and then resignedly sank back on the toilet. *Hopefully someone notices I'm missing at supper. Send out a posse to find me before my cheeks sear to the plastic!*

"Jarvis? Jarvis! You alright?" a sharp voice shouted into his little apartment.

"God, not Shirley." he groaned. "Damn, I forgot to shut the apartment door. Yea, I'm fine. Just waiting for the nurse to come and wipe my ass." He hoped that would scare her away, but he could hear the encroaching swish of shoes across the carpet like a lioness trying to sneak up on its prey.

"Like to keep the door cracked open so I get visitors," he chastised silently. "And this is what I get. The woman is a menace."

"I used to be a phlebotomist. I handled a lot of poop samples in my time. C-diff. You know, things like that."

"No, I'll wait for the nurse," Jarvis shouted. "But thanks for the offer."

"Nonsense," Shirley said as her body curled through the doorway.

"God, no! You don't have to do this," he barked, hands fig leafed over the front of the toilet. He felt a swathe of embarrassment sweep across his face and neck.

"Now Jarvis, I've seen plenty of derrieres in my time. I'm a professional." She reached across him and pushed the alarm button off. "Won't need this now. Just stand up. I'm going to use this hand towel. Clean you up in one swipe. You'll thank me later."

"But you were a phlebotomist," Jarvis said, "Why would you see plenty of derrieres?"

"I didn't say I was working at the time," Shirley answered. "Now stand up."

"Oh. Ohh!" Jarvis said in an octave of sudden insight. He snugged his hands closer to his skin as he straightened up off the seat with Shirley pulling on his good side.

"Now let me see. There, done, just as I told you. Aren't you glad I came by?" she asked dropping the towel in the garbage, and then washing her hands.

"Uh, yea," Jarvis said sheepishly. *The Navy never prepared me for this,* he thought.

"Call me anytime. Just across the hall." she warned. Leaning closer to him, she whispered, "Nice tush," and winked. Then turning around, she scooted out of the apartment.

"Not fast enough," Jarvis observed. He dropped his shorts in the garbage and washed his hands. "Glad my normal color is coming back," he said staring into the mirror. "God, that was embarrassing. Been a long time since any woman besides Molly saw my butt, well except for the nurses. Guess I still have a nice one," he said giving himself a smirky congratulations.

Fifteen minutes later unredeemable musings swept away any leftover humiliation. *Presume I don't have to worry about exposing myself in Heaven. Probably like it was supposed to be in the Garden before Eve offered Adam the apple. But what was he expected to say to a woman whose breasts were shoved in his face? Ah, no thank you, but I'll have two of those to go.*

CHAPTER TWENTY

"This seems like a waste of my time," Jarvis grumbled as his fingers crept slowly up the wall like a spider deciding where to spin its web. I could have done this at home."

Got to loosen the shoulder up first. Get the blood circulating, he could hear the therapist telling him a few moments before the man's attention had trailed over to the attractive young lady escorting another old guy out of the room.

Probably didn't hear a damn word I said. Sorry my ass isn't that good looking. Jarvis rolled his eyes and smeared disgruntlement across his face. "Hey Aaron, when are we going to get to the heavier exercises? I mean, I'd like to be out of this building before the next lunar eclipse."

The therapist rewarded him with a gruff, "funny," and then, "let's use these five pound weights to start and do some lateral raises."

"Five pounds? At least ten!"

"Five," Aaron said with arrogant inflection and thrusting the dumbbells in front of him.

Jarvis's frown morphed into a grimace by the time he reached the ninth repetition. *Must be out of shape. Not going to let him know how tough this is. Won't give him the satisfaction.*

Maybe it was just a clash of personalities, or Aaron's cavalier attitude, or the combination which irritated Jarvis, but right from the beginning the therapist's questionable stories, and what appeared to be embellished truths invited Jarvis's skepticism. *Sure hope he knows what he's doing with this therapy business!*

During their first session it was skeet shooting from the bow of a ship. "The girlfriend I was dating at the time asked me to go with her on a cruise.

Her dad was loaded," he had said very nonchalantly, like the extravagance was typical of all his relationships. "Two days in, I decided to try my luck. Never did it before. I hit every one of those clay targets. People thought I was a professional."

And then in this morning's session, Aaron had alleged he was in training to climb Mount Kilimanjaro.

"You mean the mountain in Africa?"

"That's the one. Running a mile couple times a week and lifting weights."

"Really," Jarvis said, deciding to play along with the charade. *So, you've gone from arm bending an eight ounce can of beer to a twelve ouncer. And didn't I see you smoking? Must be a new method to get in shape.* "You climb before?"

"Never. Just a natural athlete," he gloated.

"Must be," Jarvis agreed flippantly. *A regular Walter Mitty. You just gave me another incentive to get out of this place.*

Sitting in the armchair in his room, Jarvis was thinking about the morning's laughable expose. "Aaron probably gets winded climbing stairs. Now dad could have climbed that mountain, at least the man I remember from when I was kid. Always doing pushups and pullups. Who was that guy he watched on television? Uh, Jack Lalanne.

The transient comparison with the therapist was probably the reason his father visited him during the night, in a dream which exhumed secrets that had been buried longer than Jarvis had been alive. It was the conversation they had several weeks before he announced to his folks he was joining the Navy. It took him that long to reveal his decision because he wasn't sure how his parents would react. *Technically a man but acting like a wimp.*

"So, son, graduating from college in four months. Thought about what you might like to do afterwards? Been a little close-mouthed about that. Mom and I are a little curious."

"Yea, been thinking about what I might do. Didn't have an ROTC scholarship, but most likely it will be military," Jarvis asserted. "But I haven't decided yet." His mother had gone out with some girlfriends and dared to leave the two men at home. He could sniff the liquor on his father's breath, and assumed his, was just as noticeable. The old man wasn't drunk or glassy eyed because as he put it, "Even when having a few belts, a man has always got to be aware of his surroundings," but that night the alcohol did make his dad a little loose lipped.

"That would be a good choice," his father continued. "I ever tell you of the time I came home for a few days to see family before I shipped overseas. Two surprises. Your mother told me she got a job teaching English. I thought she was going to tell me she was pregnant again. The other surprise," and he chuckled, "she was going to get a tattoo in honor of the Marine Corp." His father burped and then confessed, "Couldn't believe my ears. A little Semper Fi on her bottom."

"Uh, dad, she's my mother. Do I really need to hear this?"

"I know," he said waving off the comment. "Anyhow, I laughed because I thought she was kidding, but when her face got red, I realized what a mistake I had made. I felt stupid and embarrassed. I love your mother so much, and here she was, going to do something to show how proud she was of me. Don't remember apologizing so much to anyone in my life. I took her out a couple times before I left. Glad she forgave me by the second day."

Jarvis tilted back in his chair and rested his index and middle fingers on his temple while he contemplated the penitent man in front of him. *Tough for his father, always the soldier, and sometimes bringing it home with him. I'm only twenty-one, but maybe now is the time to tell him to leave it at the front door. Risk him kicking my ass if I am a little too forthright.* "Yea, mom really loves you too dad, but occasionally you come home and act like you're still on the base, especially with me. Knees bent at a ninety-degree angle, back straight when we eat. Clothes folded just so. We're your family, not noncoms." His legs tensed ready for a quick getaway.

The old man cleared his throat. "Jarvis, you're right. I can be intolerable at times. Need to be reminded of that." His father looked away, almost dreamy eyed, and seemingly reminiscing of something else.

Didn't kill me. At least not yet, Jarvis thought.

"I ever tell you about Operation Tiger?" his dad asked slipping back into character.

"No, I don't think so." Jarvis watched his father frown and tears teeter at the bottom of his eyes.

"I never made it ashore on D-day. Never even made it across the channel. Got injured during the rehearsal for Normandy. The landing was scheduled for a month later. The training exercise was called Operation Tiger and I was on a ship in Lyme Bay off the English coast. Nazi E boats discovered us and attacked." His father glanced away and sighed. "Around seven hundred and fifty men died, including some of my buddies. I survived with a broken arm and leg. No Operation Overlord for me. I was so depressed and ashamed, like I was responsible for what happened. And very angry. Felt I had let Eisenhower and the country down. Tough time for me." He crimped his eyes as if in pain. "Sorry for any hard times I caused you and your mom."

Jarvis leaned forward and put a hand on his dad's shoulder. "Maybe it wasn't as bad as I made it out to be. Forgiven."

The man tried to smile while he nodded his thanks.

CHAPTER TWENTY-ONE

Jarvis was sitting down by the dining hall windows, looking at the park which flanked the back of Great Expectations. There was a macadam path which skirted this side of it, and since it was Spring, a blaze of pink and red azaleas dutifully greeted everyone who used it. Couples jogging, children on skateboards, dogs being walked and sometimes deer strutting past in the morning while the residents ate their breakfast.

"Well Sam," he said to the other person at the table, "how is your day going?" Jarvis didn't expect a response and continued. "Nothing to say, huh? I thought the waffles this morning weren't bad."

The man sat in the wheelchair, not moving, but his eyes shifted toward the voice. There was a brown stain on the shirt, *probably coffee someone tried to get him to drink,* Jarvis guessed. *Crummy way to spend the last months or maybe years of your life. Hard on the* family *too. It's like everyone is being persecuted.*

"My son visited me yesterday, Sam. The girlfriend left him. Guess the strain of cooking was too much to bear. She told Michael it was a sexist expectation, despite his offer to prepare some of the meals himself. I told him better now than later. Said I also seemed unhappy. Can you believe that, in this place? He pressed up against the rear of the chair and studied Sam intently. "You'd make a good psychologist just sitting there and listening. Better than most."

"Hey, old fart, got something to show you," a voice bellowed behind him.

Scarecrow Harry, Jarvis thought rolling his eyes and shaking his head in begrudging recognition. The nickname seemed appropriate for him because his hair was usually spiked out at all angles and his shirts were usually hanging half out of his pants. *Calling us old farts. He can speak for himself. Known the guy for almost three weeks and he's crazier than I am. Must be manic or something. Needs more medication. Telling me he grabbed a copperhead and held him under water until he was dead. Bigger cojones than I have, or he's full of shit, which is probably closer to the truth.*

"Hey loudmouth, they couldn't hear you on the other side of the building," Jarvis barked mockingly. He pushed down on the chair with his good arm, reflexively cringing, in anticipation of the stabbing pain which briefly skewered him whenever he squirmed around on his butt. *What did the doc say. At least six to eight weeks to heal. In the meantime, just relax. Hey doc, I'm retired. I've never been so relaxed, although this place might push me over the edge, and today, so might this shoulder.*

He massaged it gently with his hand, and that seemed to help. "Certainly feels better than last week. Probably nag me when there's a change in the weather, just like my neck does," he groused.

It was middle of the afternoon, and there were only three other people, including Sam in the room. Twelve tables, and one of the nurses had deposited Sammy across from him. Deposited, because that is what some of the staff did with non compos mentus patients. Just to put them someplace according to Jarvis's observation. "Not right."

"Have a nice conversation with Mr. Heath," the nurse had said to Sammy."

Not a little condescending, Jarvis thought in cynical disbelief. Why do they hire individuals like that? He turned his attention to Harry and watched him weave slowly around the tables, and purposely avoid the other two people in the room. They always arrived early, by two hours today, and waited to scoff down the evening gruel like they hadn't eaten in weeks. It really wasn't gruel, but it might as well have been as far as Jarvis was concerned.

Once in a while, he and Harry joked that the nurses had purposely deployed them,"

"Yea, deployed," Harry confirmed. He was an Army veteran from the late fifties. "In the outer perimeter of the room because we are least likely to get lost, or trapped between tables."

"In this place, we are practically geniuses," Jarvis said.

Ironically, several days prior, a conversation between them had revealed they each feared an indiscriminate appearance of dementia, even more than a heart attack or stroke.

"I don't want to be a burden to anybody," Jarvis conceded.

"It is a nasty affliction," Harry acknowledged. "Someday, might not be so easy to navigate around this place."

"I plan on being out of here long before then," Jarvis declared. "Hey, you missed the topless girl running down the path," he remarked stoically once his friend sat down. "She had a nice pair." He watched Harry carefully for a reaction. Sam made a whiny laugh as if he understood what was said. Harry and Jarvis glanced at him in astonishment, and then at each other. "Coincidence?" Jarvis said.

Harry just grinned. "Anyhow, if that happened, you'd be on the floor with the big one."

"Big one? Not anymore. Now it's like a stubby cigar after being smoked."

"Ha, real funny, but that isn't what I meant," was the tepid response.

"I know. Kidding."

"Have some terrific news," Harry declared. "Been set up with an insulin pump. No more needles! Thank you Jesus!"

Jarvis looked askance at him. The first day the guy said he was an atheist. *What kind of nut mentions that in conversation, the first time they talk? Must think he's going to hell anyway, so...*

"Here it is," Harry announced lifting the right side of his shirt. There was a device a little larger than a cigarette package hanging from his belt. "Isn't technology great!"

"Sure, for stuff like that," Jarvis agreed begrudgingly.

"What do you mean?" Harry asked, practically goring him with suspicion."

"Technology, I don't trust it. The kids use Pay Pal and have been trying to get me to use it too. I'm waiting for the day it gets hacked. I'm not going to say anything. Just sit back and cross my arms. Have this "I told you so" expression on my face. Michael, my oldest, says I'm stuck in the past, and that Pay Pal is safe."

"Wait a minute," Harry said, waving his arms as if to signal a time out. "I like technology. I can face time with my family, and friends. I can google information that I should remember, but..." and he sighed almost mournfully.

"Cut the crap," Jarvis said. "You probably didn't know that much in the first place."

"Oh, and you're Mr. Rocket Science."

"I've changed a few electric sockets in my time."

"That puts you at the head of the class," Harry scoffed.

"Oh, and when you wake up at three in the morning, it's because you're thinking of ways to reinvent the wheel?"

The other man responded with a sulky expression which quickly folded into one of amazement. "What has that got to do..., how do you know when I wake up?"

"Ya idiot, everybody wakes up at three when they get our age. To pee if nothing else. And around here, there isn't much else to do except stare at the ceiling, and hope that you fall back to sleep."

His highness nodded. "I counted one hundred and fifty-two ceiling tiles."

"You counted?" Jarvis exclaimed, frowning more from the suffering Harry was putting him through than the pain in his butt or shoulder. *Maybe the secret is to sit on my ass so long it gets numb.* He let a shallow chuckle seep out. *Guess it doesn't help that these are old bones.*

Jarvis wallowed in the sudden silence. When the man was quiet, you had to take advantage of the moment. Right now, Harry looked like he was sleeping with his eyes open, oblivious of everything around him. *Dad did that sometimes. Story is, he almost scared mom to death on their honeymoon. Pounded on his chest shouting wake up. Wake up.* A gasp of amusement escaped. *Everybody's got a story. Mrs. Westfield there, three ex-husbands. What a retirement plan. Sam here, I don't remember his last name, but supposedly worked for the CIA. A real James Bond.*

I'm probably the most ordinary one in the room. But that's alright. Selling houses had its reward. Meeting all kinds of people. Guiding them through one of the biggest purchases of their life. And if it wasn't for that one house, no Molly, no Michael and Shelly. Reward enough.

He stared wistfully at Harry, and then nudged him gently with his foot. "Hey old fart, wake up."

"What? What is it?"

"No need to act dumb. It's natural for you. Ya know Harry, some people believe that getting old consists of lots of pills, hip and knee surgeries, and the ability to think just cascading away. I try to act as young as possible. The kids advise me to slow down and enjoy every moment. You earned it."

"Sounds like they're expecting you to keel over any minute." They both laugh. "Have to think young to survive," Harry continued. "But someday...," he nodded thoughtfully, "hope it happens in my sleep. No pain. Just permanently out for the count, and a silly ass grin on my face."

"No argument here. None of that pounding on the chest or sending volts of electricity through my heart. I decided long ago cremation is the way to go. And don't perch my urn near a spice rack."

"What? You don't want to be seasoning in grandma's chicken soup?"

Jarvis shook his head. "I don't think I would make it taste any better. She already was a good cook. I just hope I provided Molly's life with a little spice." He yawned. "Enough talk. Maybe some shuteye before supper."

Sometimes Jarvis was fortunate enough to sleep the whole night without dreaming, or at least not able to remember any of them when he woke up. For whatever the reason, this particularly night he could recall only one brief pivot that was full of somnolent chuckles and loving accommodation.

It was the big 5-0 for Molly, and he had told her he was going above and beyond for her birthday. Jarvis didn't mention that above and beyond meant two thousand feet up in a hot air balloon.

"My God, the two of us in that little basket?"

"No, the three of us," Jarvis reminded her. "don't forget the pilot."

"Of course. It doesn't look much bigger than one of the liners in a cupcake pan."

"I think you're exaggerating a little bit," Jarvis returned with a bemused smile.

"What made you think I'd want to go up in one of those anyway?" She tilted her head and looked askance at him.

"Remember when we watched that segment on TV with all those colorful hot air balloons taking off. You said it was beautiful, and you'd like to experience it someday."

"Yes. Experience as in watching it with my feet on the ground. Besides, do you remember that I need Dramamine flying in an airplane? I'd go up in that thing and probably vomit on someone below saying, "Oh, isn't that pretty." No thank you."

Jarvis stepped back and briefly tugged on his bottom lip. "I just wanted to do something special for you."

"I know, and we are staying at the bed and breakfast." Molly tapped on her mouth, immersed in deep thought. "How about you go up, and when you've landed, or set down some place," she proffered glancing questioningly at her husband, "we go to a couple of wineries in the area." There was a finality to her proposition.

"Well, it is your birthday," Jarvis said. "Guess we should do that."

"Maybe we can get back to the B&B early," his wife said with a hint of intended prurience.

"Yes, let's definitely do that," he quickly agreed.

CHAPTER TWENTY-TWO

Sally Kimble was one of the nurses who gave Jarvis his medicine. A cute girl, with captivating blue eyes, and a blithesome spirit that could roust the humor out of the crankiest patients. She also happened to be seven months pregnant, although looking at her, Jarvis thought the doctors had miscalculated the due date. She appeared much further along according to his expert observation. *Wasn't around much when Molly was pregnant because of my deployment, but I saw Shelly with the boys. Don't think I could have gotten my arms around either of them, especially Shelly when she was nine months.*

A week ago, he had been sitting in the lounge reading a magazine when Sally came in to dispense the white tablet for his blood pressure, and the two vitamins. He heard a squeal, and out of the corner of his eye, saw the woman slip, and list backwards with arms flailing, reaching out for something that would prevent her from striking the floor. He was sure she would have fallen completely, and maybe hurt the baby if he hadn't lunged forward and caught her on the way down. "Instinct and adrenaline kicked in simultaneously," he told Harry. "No time to think. Just act. Hard to believe I can still move that quickly. Glad I didn't injure myself again."

Presently, he and Sally were sitting at the front of the Dining Hall. She was sipping apple juice, and he was having his ritual 10 a..m. coffee. Jarvis concluded she felt some overriding obligation to sit with him as a sign of appreciation. "But it's not necessary," he explained to her. "You don't owe me anything. If I was pregnant, you would have done the same."

"If you were pregnant, I would want part of your book proceeds," she replied.

"Ha. Very funny," was Jarvis's feeble response.

Nurse Kimble, as he affectionately called her, reminded him of his daughter when she was pregnant, and so he charitably slid into the role of a third *Pops, well,* in his mind anyway. *"My craziness allows me to believe any fantasy I want."*

"Thanks for letting me spend a few minutes with you Jarvis."

"My pleasure. You and the baby okay?"

Sally glanced down at her belly. I think Alex and I are doing fine."

"Boy, huh?"

"Yes. Found out the other day. Now I know how to decorate the nursery. Be a surprise for my parents when they visit." A pregnant glow brightened her face.

"This is our first time," she said patting herself. "My husband is so excited. "However, the baby is not so tiny anymore, and he's become very protective. Doesn't want me to work. Afraid to touch me too. Thinks I'll break." She frowned. "I miss the closeness." She giggled nervously. "So sorry Mr. Heath. I shouldn't be telling you any of this."

"Don't worry," Jarvis said reassuringly. "You'd be amazed what people have said while I'm driving them around to see houses. I was a realtor for many, many years."

"You do have a trusting face."

"I'm kind also," he joked. "A real boy scout."

Sally laughed. "I believe it." They each took a sip of their drinks, and then Sally glanced at her watch. "Gotta go Jarvis. Thanks for the company" She put a hand on top of his shoulder. "You're a good friend."

"Uh, thanks. "Need any help getting up?"

"No, I'll be fine."

Watching her move awkwardly out of the chair, and down the hall, reminded Jarvis that he had only seen his wife's waddling walk a few times because he had been doing the touristy thing the military liked to encourage, and serving two tours of duty in Vietnam when she was pregnant with each of their kids. Amazingly, Uncle Sam allowed him to come home for Christmas, see his daughter for the first time, and then do his part to see that she had a brother or sister.

"What was the opening line in Tale of Two Cities, "It was the best of times, it was the worst of times, or something like that."

Jarvis clasped his hands behind his head and leaned back. He chuckled and let a smile spring to his face as he recalled the experience with Shelly the first time she was ready to deliver one of his grandsons.

She had called a taxi, when the contractions got bad. *"No Uber back then,"* he jocularly reminded himself. *"What a generation. I apparently wasn't important enough to be called ahead of a taxi!"*

"I'll be right over."

"No daddy. Just meet me at the hospital.

"Where's Larry?" *"The bum of a husband, and not around when she needed him,"* he thought. *"I couldn't help being six thousand miles away when Molly needed me."*

"Probably fighting traffic, and cussing. He said he'd be here within the hour."

"Within the hour! And what about your mother?"

"She's teaching dad. The school has to find a substitute."

"Oh, that's right."

"Be calm dad. You're going to be fine."

"Yea, I know. Just concerned about my baby girl, and my, err, grandchild.'

"I know. There's honking. Gotta go. See you at the hospital."

"Ahh, that Larry." Jarvis grumbled, as he struggled to shift his position in the chair. His weak legs had gotten stronger with time and therapy, but sitting for so long stiffened them up. "Not the guy I would have chosen for her, but not my decision. All these years, and I still don't understand why Shelly married him. Oh yes, how silly of me. Perfect hair, beguiling eyes and broad shoulders. Glad Molly didn't judge me by those standards, although I guess I was kind of handsome back then."

"Daddy, he's an accountant. He'll always have a job," his daughter recounted defensively the only time he had put up a fuss. "And we love each other so much." And she still believed that after the two years they had been living together. That's what he found remarkable. She was apparently blind to everything else.

"From what you complain about, and your mother and I see when we visit, he should have been a sportscaster." That always brought a smudge of annoyance to his daughter's face.

"Yes, he watches a lot of football, and basketball, but that will change after we're married."

And it did, Jarvis had to admit, *especially after the boys came. However, there was the money issue. He spent it like he was printing it in the basement.*

"Daddy, you're impossible!"

"I'm sorry. Just looking out for my little girl. I'll never bring it up again."

Jarvis shook his head. In the beginning he hadn't known about the mantra Larry lived by, keeping up with Jones, and apparently neither had Shelly, or she purposely ignored it. However, after the first invitation to the in-laws, and seeing how they lived, he should have surmised it might turn into a problem.

For Shelly, that meant a new house every five to six years, new vehicles, country club memberships, and the ever-evolving debt she had begun to complain about. "But that isn't your concern," Molly kept reminding him, "and you did make that promise to her."

"I know," he would admit with a slight nod of his head., "Glad you're a one house girl."

"And you, in real estate," she would return. "Think we could have moved once in all these years. I think we can afford it."

"Just because we can, doesn't mean we have to spend the money. Besides, we love this neighborhood, and it's so convenient to town."

"Mr. Scrooge," she murmured, loud enough for him to hear.

"We have something many people don't have."

"And what's that?"

"Each other."

Molly shook her head, and unsuccessfully attempted to restrain the reflexive smile that wedged her lips up at the corners. "You, should have been a politician," she said pointedly.

Later, Jarvis was sitting in the media room, with its large sixty-six inch screen, and three computer stations. There was an old murder mystery yelling back at him from the television because the other two individuals in the room were hard of hearing. At the moment, their competing snores were so loud, he could barely hear the movie actors speaking, and he never did learn to read lips. He took the remote and aimed it like a weapon at the set. Abruptly, there was one less clamoring blast assaulting his ears. He aimed it at the two old ladies who shared the sofa, and like magic, one of them stopped her snoring.

"Now that, is power," Jarvis proclaimed quietly. "Hope she's still breathing."

The ebbing tempest of sounds allowed taunting weariness to seduce him, and soon he found himself in a neighborhood of familiarly quaint, craftsman like style homes, and white picket fences. He had installed a lockbox on one house, and was stepping off the porch when a high pitched, helpless voice called out to him.

"Oh mister, would you get Henry out of the tree?" On the sidewalk next door was a thin, older woman with cottony white hair, and she was pointing toward a tree in her yard.

"Mister, would you get Henry out of the tree." she repeated more emphatically.

"Henry? Who's Henry?" Jarvis asked. *Is her husband up there?*" He peered into the tangly mesh of green leaves and branches.

"My cat Henry. He can be such a nuisance sometimes. He's a vagabond."

"A vagabond?"

"I do a lot of reading. Now could you climb up there and grab him."

"Won't I scare him further up the tree?"

"Believe it or not, he's afraid of heights. Anything above twenty feet, and his paws stay glued to the branch. That's why he is meowing."

"Ah, yes. I can hear him now." Jarvis said approaching the woman. "Can't see him yet," but he couldn't resist the crinkly face, and the twinkle in her eyes. "I'll get him for you." He started to climb the tree and was thankful the branches were staggered like rungs all the way to the top.

"Am I really doing this?" he murmured disbelievingly. "I drove out because I'm selling the house next door." A third of the way up, he saw Henry, tawny colored with white splotches, studiously watching his every move. "Come to me," Jarvis pleaded as he reached over and curled his hand beneath the cat. Henry meowed once, and then willingly surrendered to his rescuer.

"Some cat you have here," Jarvis said when he was back on the ground.

"Henry's an adventurer. Doesn't think though and gets himself in such predicaments."

"You and Henry live alone?"

"Of course not. We have friends inside. Would you like to meet them?"

"Well, I only have a few minutes," Jarvis said even as the old woman turned and started up the walk. "Say, what's your name?" he asked catching up to her.

"Sylvia," she said opening the front door.

Immediately a crescendo of meows, and a visible scurrying of furry feet caught Jarvis's attention. So did the smell of a manure covered field, except it was coming from inside the house. He kept wriggling his nose hoping to palliate the odor. *"This place stinks. How can she live here?"* he questioned. He nearly stepped into one of the two litter boxes just inside the door. "How many cats do you have?"

"About eight," Sylvia said dropping Henry to the floor.

Jarvis thought it was funny that being a male cat he wiggled his ass like he was one of the ladies, then, "Eight!"

"I think so. Maybe ten. I love them all."

"I'm sure you do. But aren't they difficult to take care of?" A gray and white cat rubbed up against Jarvis's leg, and meowed. "Cute face," he thought as it looked up at him. "And thanks for the fur," he said looking at his pants. "Anyone check in on you? Any children?"

"No, just me and all my friends." She beamed like a proud parent.

"Hate to do it," Jarvis griped silently, "but I'd feel guilty if I didn't contact some agency to check on Sylvia., and her cats. Make sure the old woman can safely live by herself. The smell is bad in here, but don't see any poop on the floors. Sylvia smells like lavender, but she is kind of thin." He wrinkled his forehead in consternation. *Sorry Sylvia. Hope you don't end up in a nursing home.*

CHAPTER TWENTY-THREE

Jarvis hung his head down and sighed as he watched the eight ball roll easily into the corner pocket. "Not the one I expected to go in," he groaned.

"Letting me win again," Harry said, embracing his success with an overconfident grin.

Jarvis gave him the satisfaction of a weak smile. "Wait till I'm one hundred percent. Playing with one arm in a sling, and a broken ass gives you an advantage. Or maybe, just maybe, I'm letting you win," he said deftly. "Notice how I usually nudge a few of your balls into the pockets. Skill."

"Sure. You can believe that if you want," Harry replied, being his usual contrary, egotistical self.

Jarvis gazed at him in disbelief. "You should do Ancestry.com. I'll bet your family tree goes all the way back to Cro-Magnon man. No self-esteem issues there. Just club your food over the head and grunt a lot."

"A man's man. I'd be in good company."

"Yea, and for you, it would be a step up."

"Oh, your words scare me," Harry intoned with a flare of theatric gruffness.

The plan was for them to start playing some competitive pool, otherwise known as billiards every Monday, Wednesday, and Friday at one O'clock. Competitive, as defined by the ministrations of two youngsters trapped in old guy bodies. Afterwards, they would go back to their rooms to take naps.

Jarvis had never been good at the game and didn't expect to become a Minnesota Fats at this stage of his life. He mostly played to keep Harry at bay and satisfy the man's unrelenting bombast. As if *he would ever be cognizant of anyone making derogatory statements about him. His ego is too big.*

Shortly after he moved in, one of the residents told him Harry was the town crier, knew everybody, and their business. It didn't take long for the man to live up to his reputation.

"Watched the news this morning," Harry said as they sat down on the bench beside the table. "You know, sometimes it feels as if life is passing me by."

"Who is this dejected figure before me?" Jarvis wondered cynically.

"They were reviewing some Pop Culture stuff from the past decade and shared a 2012 music video showing a South Korean I never heard of, singing, and dancing Gangnam Style, which I also never heard of. You?"

Instead of scrunching his face into the usual, "do you think I care," put down, which was habitually ignored anyway, Jarvis tried to hide behind a less obvious display of sarcasm. "Can't say that I have. I must be missing out too."

Harry pressed his lips into a narrow line of annoyance and shook his head. "Supposedly went viral. Just can't keep up anymore."

"Don't worry my friend. You're old now, and it's forgivable to forget."

"Right smartass. Let's see how good your memory is! Ah..., you remember your first time, or was it too long ago?"

"First time I... kissed a girl?"

"No. The first time you rounded the bases," Harry said feistily.

"Almost like it was yesterday," Jarvis said proudly. "And that's the truth. Her name was Barbie, Barbara really. Blonde, full breasts, and eighteen. I was nineteen. I remember it well because I was so nervous. I really liked this girl, if infatuation counts. We had just finished eating, Italian I believe, and were already outside the restaurant when I remembered forgetting to leave a tip." Jarvis turned his hands out like what do you expect. "I was an amateur back then. I ran back in thinking the waitress would complain to her colleagues what a bum I was, or worse yet, somehow get my number and call my parents." Both men simpered at the guilty foolishness of adolescence.

"Anyhow, after I explained to Barbie what I'd done, we walked back to the car and got in. Figured I lost any chance to get to second base, or any base, especially with her in the front seat giggling about the whole thing. I didn't think it was funny at all, and just stared out the windshield."

"It's okay," she said. "Mistakes happen. She turned my head toward her and kissed me right on the mouth. Surprised the hell out of me. But I didn't need any more encouragement. The ole testosterone just kicked in.

Course back then we didn't have any internet porn to study, or Sex for Dummies. Had to wing it based on all the questionable stories, and advice I heard from my buddies. Sex ed was a waste, and actually, so were my buddies."

"Probably can get college credit in that right now," Harry interjected, "How to become an Escort or Giglio in one semester?" The gratuitous absurdity of his remarks elicited a short breach of laughter.

"Wouldn't surprise me. Dumbing down of the youth. I read there are credit courses in college that teach students how to improve their video game skills. Many kids today can't add or subtract in their heads, but they sure know how to access porn, or battle their way through an enemy encampment on a computer screen."

"That's interesting," Harry said with mocking sincerity, "but you were going to tell me more about the girl? Definitely more interesting."

"What's to tell. I had my hand up her skirt, and she had her hands in my pants." Jarvis chuckled. "The windows got all steamed up. Forgot we were still in the parking lot. But I wasn't about to stop.

Harry chuckled. "You should be glad no one tapped on your window"

"Never entered my mind," Jarvis admitted. "Anyhow, it was sort of on the job training. So inept, but in the end, hands on, got the job done."

"So, you didn't actually...?"

"Do that? Nah, but we were both happy enough with the way things ended."

Your turn to confess, Harry oh boy, but it'll have to wait till next time. Going to get a few minutes of shuteye. Besides, give you time to think up a big whopper. Can't wait to hear it."

"Hey, you won't believe your ears."

"Yea, I'm sure you're right" Jarvis agreed, already doubting Harry's veracity.

As he walked down the hall to his room, a vein of doubt undermined any desire for sleep. The day before it was a similar scene, where the inviting promise of sleep abruptly deserted him, and he lay on the bed for an hour with his eyes closed, and his hands tucked neatly behind his head, awake." *Hope that doesn't happen today. Didn't sleep well last night either. Maybe today will be better. A good massage might help. Not Aaron. Don't want those hands on me. Maybe one of the nurses. Just my neck and shoulders. A beer too, ha. Sounds so relaxing.* Jarvis suddenly chuckled when the figure of his wife in a sexy nightgown popped into his head. *Now that woman could get me to relax.* He shook his head, his eyes bright with wanton recollection. *Funny how one word can get my imagination to run wild.* "One track mind," *Molly would say. After all these years, I'm beginning to agree with her.*

"Blame the testosterone, and your sexy body," he would whisper kissing her neck. He would wrap his arms just below her breasts, and pull her closer, so his groin rubbed up against her backside.

"You are impossible. Give me ten minutes, and I'll see you in the bedroom, mister." Then she usually peeked over her shoulder at him with this carnal glint in her eyes, and he would do a little dance down the hallway.

Jarvis kicked his shoes off and lay gently down on the bed like he was porcelain and might break. "The therapy does seem to be helping," he mumbled, "but these old bones are taking their time to heal."

He closed his eyes, waiting for the provocative image of his wife to reappear, but all that flashed into his mind was a scene from many years ago. He was mentioning to her some ridiculous poll that had been taken about people's sex lives. "Can you believe this? Individuals were asked how often they do it, not very credible. I bet everybody lies a little bit. This couple says they do it six times a week. We only do it five? Wow, here's a husband who claims ten times a week. But my favorite, "we actually get disability because we don't have the energy to get out of bed. I'm sure they're joking."

Molly peeked over at him. "I'd be burying you if we did it any more often."

"Huh, not true!"

Jarvis studied the white, popcorn ceiling. "Maybe this will make me drowsy. It's so dull. Count the tiles like Harry said he did."

But after a few impatient minutes, he turned his head to the side and grumbled, "Never going to sleep," The photo album was on the bedside table, and he reached over to grab it. Unfortunately, the combination of age and debility had sapped the youthful strength in his arms, and the heavy book pulled him upright as he dragged it over. Propping himself up, he opened to the bent down corner. It was a habit that never made his wife happy.

"How many times do I have to tell you? Don't bend the pages. Not difficult." Or her other tact, "don't you want to please me. It's just a little thing."

Molly was the one who did all the photography in the family.

Professional like. He told her several times she should work for National Geographic.

"I'd always be away from you and the kids. I'd miss you so much." She'd look at him with those sad panda bear eyes of hers, and they'd end up on the carpet, squirming around like two teenagers. *Yep, one track mind.*

There were photos of their Niagara Falls trip. They stayed on the Canadian side. The American side was shameful. A smile set on his face, and his shoulders slumped comfortably in remembrance. *That was a great vacation.* One of many they took after the kids were finally out of the house, although Shelly did move back briefly. She discovered incriminating texts on her boyfriend's phone, the one she had before she met her husband. She was twenty-six and devastated. But being strong willed, she rallied her spirit and eventually fell in love again and got married this time.

Jarvis had seen pictures of the Falls, but being there magnified their awesome power. "Take some real cojones to go over those in a barrel, or a death wish." They were on the Maid of the Mist tour that brought visitors as close to the falls as possible. The guide was telling them about some of the people who had foolishly tried, and the twelve who did survive.

The spray from the pulverizing crash of the water as it hit bottom soaked the rain gear the boat operators had given all of them to wear. Molly did one of those silly things that tourists do sometimes, and pretended she was on the Titanic with her body stretched out over the railing, just like in the movie. He held on to her real tight, more afraid she would fall in than she probably was. One of the guides yelled at them. "What's he going to do?" he asked her. "Have us walk the plank, or give us our money back?"

"Probably take us to the Canadian police, and we won't be allowed back into the states." Molly replied, dropping back down.

That night after eating dinner on the veranda of some restaurant nudged up against the St Lawrence, they strolled hand in hand to the banister and fell in love with all the lights glittering on the Niagara River.

"So romantic," Molly murmured.

"Magic," Jarvis said, and hugged her closer.

Chapter Twenty-Four

"Damn sciatica!" Jarvis growled as he pressed down on the arms of the chair and shifted his weight over to the other cheek. "I want to get out of this place. Been here long enough! The walls of this room are closing in."

After a few minutes, the pain decreased like it usually did when he relieved the pressure on his right leg. "You punishing me?" he angrily asked, glancing resentfully upward. "Sorry! But it's been two months! My shoulder is stronger," and he rotated it slowly around to prove it. "And my butt feels better, well, until this nerve thing happened." He crossed his arms defiantly in front of him, and made this deep, throaty noise like a bull just before it charges. Then, unexpectedly, he surrendered a smile after a wake of insight washed over him. "Maybe I'll play with the truth a little bit. Tell the doc no problem reaching my butt to wipe it, and this new leg and cheek pain, hardly know it's there. Not going to let something like that keep me here any longer. He snickered, and then shook his head haplessly. "My penance is over," and then winced as the sharp sting cut briefly into his leg.

He knew plans had already been made for him to go back to the house, but now the crippling sear of pain periodically forced him to use the railings to work his way down the hall. "I can use the furniture at home to support myself," he snarled convincingly to himself.

"I'll call a taxi and sign myself out," Jarvis told Harry later that morning. "I'm of sound mind." They were both sitting in the Adirondack chairs guarding the front entrance to the Assisted Living.

"Were you ever of sound mind?" Harry asked.

"Absolutely not," Jarvis replied indignantly. "My record speaks for itself."

His friend chuckled. "My man, your body is slowly disintegrating from the inside out."

Jarvis leaned back with his hands behind his head and a presumptive grin smeared across his face. "Like my father's antique car, a 1926 Ford Model T if I remember correctly, inherited from an uncle who died in his thirties. The exterior looked pretty good, and polished, you'd think he spent hours every week taking care of that car.

Truth is, my father never maintained the engine. So if the hood was lifted, there would be a lot of gagging, and walking away. My grandson would say that was a, fail." Both men muffled a laugh. "They speak a language we're not supposed to understand."

"Kids. What will they think of next?" Harry remarked. "Say, speaking of automobiles, remember when you could play with the flutter valve to get a car started? And changing the oil filter was so simple."

Jarvis chuckled. "Yea, and now, instead of just sliding the wiper blades in and out when they need changing, it requires a special tool. What? Just to make a few extra bucks." They were sitting on the veranda, enjoying the cool whisper of air from the fan overhead, and reminiscing about anything that happened to insinuate itself into their rumination. Whatever the nurses had given him for the Sciatica was working overtime, and Jarvis couldn't have been happier.

"Did you ever think the day would come when there would be a charge to put air in your tires?" Harry asked.

"Or pay four to five dollars for a coffee and wait for it in a line that snaked around the building," Jarvis exclaimed incredulously. "Times sure have changed." He made this guttural exhalation that would have frightened any child and jammed his hands against the wood hoping to shift his less than agile body just a few inches. Harry watched with bemusement and didn't say anything.

Jarvis frowned. "These Adirondacks are impossible. It's like prying myself out of the car after driving for three hours, the body all cramped up, and achy. Think they'd get a pair of rockers for us old timers, instead of these contraptions." He pushed down again, and with a herculean grunt, finally scooted his butt over. He and Harry were sunk into the jaw of the chairs and kept sliding backward whenever they tried to escape them. "Seems like it's trying to swallow me." he said.

"Long as we're paying customers, they'll do anything to make us stay, including flesh eating chairs.," Harry said. "Hmm, new pet peeve. You have any?"

Jarvis's eyes lit up like he had received a gift. "Are you kidding. I'm seventy-five. What do you think?"

"Well..."

"Hundreds of them, but traffic has got to be one of the aggravating. Worse than these damn chairs."

Harry slapped his thigh and grinned. "Me too."

"Yea. It made Molly crazy, or rather, guess I did. She never understood my frustration. Backed up for miles. No accident. No road construction. "Have patience," she'd shout at me.

Harry nodded almost gleefully. "I used words which guaranteed me twenty-four hours of no sex. Sometime forty-eight. Wife hated foul language."

"Uh-huh. Reason I did a lot of home projects when Molly wasn't around. Anyway, the truth as I see it," Jarvis said raising a hand to make his point, "is that two or three smart-alecky drivers deliberately travel beside each other at the same slow speed, backing up all the vehicles behind them. Gives them a sense of power."

"You figured that out, huh?"

"I was awarded a Noble Peace Prize. Years in the making to figure it out."

"Clever," Harry replied sarcastically.

"Got another one," Jarvis continued, like an excited school kid who knows all the answers. "Vasectomies. Another pain in the ass, or in this case, pain in the balls. What man wants one?"

"Not me," Harry interrupted. "Makes me cringe just thinking about it."

"I had one," Jarvis confessed. "Like being kicked between the legs over and over and that was after the shot to numb the area. The doc finally said, "I'm done," and boy, did I breathe a sigh of relief. Then he said, "Now I'm going to do the other side."

I wanted to punch him, but he was holding these sharp instruments in his hands. So, I just asked, "what do you mean?"

"You have two testicles."

"Crap." I remember looking up, and muttering, "You couldn't give us just one?" I cried like a baby when the Doc was all done. Like a piece of my manhood had been torn away."

"So how come you got one?"

"Sore subject that popped up, so to speak, after Michael was born. Molly gave me an ultimatum, vasectomy or no sex."

"Not to insult your wife, but that doesn't sound like much of a choice. Why didn't she have it done while she was in the hospital?"

"Complications with the pregnancy. Ah, really high blood pressure. And I figured after two pregnancies, seemed fair I be the one to get snipped."

"Sounds like the doc used a pair of garden shears," Harry offered, tacitly dropping his hands down to cover himself.

"Felt like it. Doing it for the team."

"Think I'd ask to be traded. But at least you could have sex without worrying about another kid."

"Same sort of reasoning Molly used. Would have been nice to have when I was single, and then order replacement parts when I got married. Sad thing is, lost much of my desire to get any since she passed."

Later, after his afternoon medication, Jarvis returned to his room, and lay on the bed. Only two *pills, and they won't trust me* with *the bottles? Another reason to leave.* He sighed with frustration, as snippets from the morning's conversation breached his brooding manner, and disinterred a witless humiliation which he had buried many years before.

Men do stupid things, sometimes, he qualified silently. Then to the Man upstairs, *Thanks for helping me find my way. I need it once in a while.*

"Traffic. Endless traffic," Jarvis yelped with a disbelieving shake of his head. "We've been stopped here for forty-five minutes! The line seems to go on forever, or at least over the top of the next hill!" Heavy rain had already brandished its wrath and put Molly and him an hour behind. "Now this!" A litany of invectives lapped upon his tongue, but with difficulty, he managed to reign them in. Instead, he looked over at his wife sitting behind the wheel, and inflicted her with a blatant display of disgust, as if the traffic was her fault.

She glowered at him, and retorted, "I didn't plan this. All we can do is ride it out!"

"Ride it out, ha. That would be fine if we were moving. But we're not. All I see are brake lights for miles. I'm not happy. I bet I could reach the

top of the hill before the car does. Anyhow, I need to walk off some steam."
He unhooked the seatbelt and put his hand on the door lock.

"Jarvis! You're not going to...?"

"I am."

"You could get killed!"

"I'll be safe on the shoulder. Your grandmother moves faster than these vehicles are moving, and she uses a walker. Hell, I wouldn't be surprised if other people get out, and follow me."

The moment the passenger door slammed behind him, Jarvis regretted his decision. *Look up idiot in the dictionary, and you'll find my name.* He walked to the front of the car and stopped, wondering why common sense had abandoned him. *I've done crazy things, but this is nuts. I hope Molly doesn't divorce me.* He peeked warily through the windshield to see if she appeared angry. Instead, his wife looked bewildered, and scared. And that was enough incentive to retrace his steps and slide back in beside her.

There was no talking until they returned home, just unbearably, hostile silence. Whenever Jarvis did try to speak, Molly shoved her palm in his face. So, it was with thankful relief, he accepted the chastising lashes she delivered after they went into the house.

"I'm not going to ask for a divorce, I love you too much. However, are you out of your mind?! I was so frightened! What if a vehicle pulled out of traffic, and you were in a blind spot? What if there had been an accident, and rescue vehicles needed to get through?" Her hands shook as she curled them into claws that could rake his face. "You make me so..." she sputtered. "Do all men have this defective gene in their chromosomes?

"Was very stupid of me," Jarvis admitted. He sighed and crushed his expression into one of remorse. "So, so sorry." *And I truly am,* he thought resolutely.

"It may be a while before I can accept your apology," Molly said, her voice strewn with a blend of irritation, and hurt. "I don't want to have any more discussions. No excuses. Nothing! I'll let you know when I'm feeling better about this whole situation."

Two days later they kissed on the lips. Three days after that they made love.

But it was within the genre of near-death experiences, by vehicle, or by wife, real or imagined, that another dream unfolded, and pulled Jarvis back into a story line that was about twenty-five years old. One in which he was sure divine intervention had been responsible for keeping him alive.

It had been a windless morning, with the baking heat of summer already cuddling his body with its steamy blanket. A fine day for the family to be out on the water. The plan was for them to have a fun, relaxing time rafting down a local river, and then have friends bring them back to the SUV about two hours later. However...

"Didn't expect this," Jarvis groaned watching the frothy waters in front of him. He stood akimbo and stared pensively at the rushing current. "It rained heavily yesterday, but this is more than the usual rapids."

He turned and studied each of the faces behind him. "Still game?"

"Let's do it," Michael shouted, apparently not too concerned with the height of the churning waves.

"If you say so, dad," Shelly said hesitantly. Her eyes appeared wide from fright more than any anticipated excitement.

Molly was critically assessing the rushing water, and furtively glancing at him. "I don't know Jarvis. Seems kind of dangerous. Are we experienced enough for this?"

That had been ten minutes before, and now the raft was being tossed around with four grimly faced passengers holding on for their lives. *God, big mistake*, Jarvis thought fearfully. *This isn't just me, landing a jet with a snapped arresting cable. This is my family.* He lurched forward as the raft was thrust up like a sounding whale, and then slammed back down with a loud splat. "Everybody hang on!" he yelled, checking that everyone was on board.

"What do you think we're doing?" Molly shouted back at him.

Jarvis grunted his gratitude and pointed to a section of the embankment jutting out like a peninsula. "Let's try paddling over there," he yelled as bucket like dumps of water kept washing over them.

A few moments later he realized they were caught in a large eddy in the middle of the river. "Yea, this is working," he muttered, and then suddenly cried out as the raft careened against a mountainous wave that lifted them all up in the air and pushed him over the side.

Screams of "Daddy! Daddy!" and "Jarvis! Oh my God, Jarvis!" accosted him as he tightened his grip on the rope tied into the edge of the raft.

"Can't die in front of them," Jarvis grunted as a swirling white cap smashed his face, and jagged boulders scraped his back and legs. *Got to keep my head up. Can't be sucked under!*

Immediately he felt a strong grip on his left wrist, and Michael shouting, "Dad, I've got you. Pull!"

And then providentially, a random wave popped Jarvis up, and Michael jerked him in. "Dad! Duck! We're headed into the branches of a downed tree!"

"Grab one," Jarvis stammered, fighting the tremor of exhaustion which suddenly came over him. He forced himself to reach up, and grab a limb, anything he might find useful to help haul the family to safety. "Gotch ya," he cried out, mustering some latent strength as he gripped a leafy twig, and began sliding his hand down toward a thicker part of the branch. "I'm so weak," he mumbled, trying to shake off the insistent splatter of water soaking all of them. "Have to hang on."

"Got one!" Michael yelled.

"Michael, I've got one too! Help me pull us in," Molly shouted. "We're not far from shore!"

Jarvis kept clinging to different parts of the tree as he watched his wife, Michael, and now Shelly, moving the raft slowly closer to the embankment.

"There!" Molly shouted. "Michael, grab your father!" and suddenly Jarvis felt the tug of his son, and pushed off on weakened legs until they both were able to drag themselves off the raft.

"Made it. We're all alive," Jarvis gasped. Legs *feel like I've been running stadium steps*. He glanced at his wife, "Tomorrow's already better than today," he whispered. "I've still got you beside me."

"I'm not letting you get away that easily mister," Molly replied.

Chapter Twenty-Five

There was no room for the virus on his schedule. The nursing home and rehab section were doing their part to stop its intrusion, by recently locking down, and not letting anyone but masked staff, into the building. *It's like Halloween twenty-four hours a day*, Jarvis thought facetiously, *but with consequences that could be dire*, he finished somberly.

Outside the walls of Great Expectations Covid was wreaking havoc, insinuating itself into people's lives, and keeping loved ones apart. *So far, nothing inside this place*, he admitted gratefully, but the looming threat rankled him, igniting wrathful condemnation. *I'll be damned if that thing is going to stop me from getting out of here. I'm going home in three more days. Freedom.*

A caretaker would visit him for an hour every day, making sure he took his medicine. "Why wouldn't I?" And ate correctly. "What's wrong with peanut butter and jelly sandwiches?" And washed himself. "Maybe she would take a shower with me."

But the virus was on its own schedule, and devious, with no willingness to abide by Jarvis's calendar. Its assault had begun in China, subtle at first, but just something happening over there. Maybe some biological weapon gone terribly wrong according to the rumor mill. Nobody knew for sure. And then it reared its ugly head and attacked with a malice that indiscriminately mauled mostly middle aged and older adults all over the world.

Jarvis and Harry were in the TV room, with its sixty-six inch flatscreen, the sound turned down low so they could hear each other speak. They were sitting six feet apart, just like the nurses directed them, and had their masks on because of the newly implemented policy. "Can't trust you two characters," one of them affectionately teased.

"What? Think we'll lock lips after you leave?" Jarvis joked. He was jubilant, and nothing was going to stymie his departure. But after she left, the aura of optimism was clouded by the appearance of the President and some of his staff on the television screen.

"God. Thousands dying every day, and our omniscient leader twiddling his thumbs," Jarvis muttered.

"I guess you're being sarcastic," Harry said. "I know your love for the man doesn't exactly run deep."

"Runs into the swampy, muck of incompetence."

"Well, if that's what you want to believe," Harry said begrudgingly, but from my perspective. . ."

"No buts Harry, unless you're talking about from whence which body part he speaks. The only person who matters to him is the one staring back from the mirror. But I don't want to argue. You're my best friend." Harry coughed, and then lowering his mask, atomized the air with a forceful sneeze.

"How long have you been doing that?" Jarvis asked, cautiously.

"Two, three days. Nothing to be worried about. My grandson visited about a week ago. He had a cold. He's been out of school for two weeks and taking classes online. Said his mother's been coaching him, and he's glad she isn't his regular teacher." He chuckled, and then coughed again.

Jarvis leaned away and froze his face in a mask of phobic suspicion. "You have a temperature?"

"Nope. No difficulty breathing either. Appetite a little less. Probably good for me. So, no virus. Satisfied?"

"Only if you have the test." Jarvis said pushing himself off the sofa. "I like ya Harry, but I'm not taking any chances. Not with three days left. Maybe you ought to have that checked out." He didn't expect the rebuking glare cast back at him.

"Really! Come on Jarvis! You know I'd be quarantined in my room."

"Harry, I'm surprised. You'd rather contaminate everybody, then be examined for the virus?"

"Look, I don't have it!" Harry replied with undisguised annoyance.

Jarvis frowned when he saw the depth of his neighbor's defiance and belligerent angst. But according to the news, his billiard buddy was hardly the only one who believed in their invincibility, or even the reality of the disease. *"I just don't want to become one of the statistics,"* he thought grimly. *And I want to get home.* He crimped his lips together in consternation before speaking. "Harry, I just want to stay healthy."

"Don't worry," his neighbor growled. "You'll get home!" Jarvis watched him swipe his forehead with the back of his hand. "Must have the heat on," Harry muttered, rebuffing Jarvis's ardent stare. "Going back to my room to rest." He pushed himself out of the chair, staggered, and then recovered well enough to disappear down the hall.

That evening, a nurse, masked, gloved and gowned took his temperature, and told him he would have to stay in the room. "Your meals will be brought to you." she said.

"No fever, so what's the big deal?" he asked.

The nurse leaned back through the doorway. "I'm not supposed to tell you this, but you and Harry are friends. We had to send him to the hospital. We're keeping everyone isolated." Three hours later Jarvis was transferred to the hospital because he was having trouble breathing.

Every time he exhaled, his lungs made this crackling noise, much like the sound he used to make when he was a kid blowing air through a straw into his milkshake.

"Hey, trouble breathing here," Jarvis shouted in his head, but it came out only as a whisper, the tight breathing mask over his mouth and nose further muffling whatever sound he made. Desperately, he reached over his head, and searched for the knob that controlled the oxygen. When he found it, he turned it clockwise, just like he had seen the nurse do. "Better." he gasped.

He had been in the intensive care for twelve hours and he was getting worse. His ribs looked like sculpted relief on the sides of his chest. And the bellows like breathing was taxing his energy and forcing beads of sweat on his forehead. The added oxygen seemed to help a little bit, but Jarvis worried it was just a figment of his imagination, because the hugging heaviness remained in his chest.

Feels like a boulder on top of me. Getting tired. Too much work. The terrifying thoughts tripped over each other. His eyes flit anxiously to the glass doors in front of him.

I've got so much more living to do, he implored, peering upward and quietly pleading his case. *Lord, I know you make all the really big decisions because God knows, well, we humans screw up even the little ones.*

But maybe there'll be another grandchild, or maybe a cure for aging. Haven't seen the Pyramids yet. Something Mollie and I wanted to do. Can you give me another chance? Search up your sleeves and pull off another miracle.

He waited a few moments for a response. "No, huh?" Jarvis panted. Even that with a laborious effort. *"Time for me to do my part,"* he conceded tacitly.

Abruptly a group of four gowned and masked individuals entered the room, leaving some kind of alien looking machine with knobs and dials and hoses in the doorway.

"The bank is down the street," Jarvis wanted to joke, but each breath required his full attention.

"Mr. Heath, we need to intubate you. To put a tube down your throat and into your lungs." one of the disguised members said with curt abruptness.

The doctor I presume, Jarvis thought. Then, orchestrating every word, "Do I have a choice?"

"No. If we don't do this, you will die."

Seems like a crass way to put it, Jarvis bandied back in his head. "How many of those machines do you have," he whispered, each shallow breath an exhausting struggle. He nodded slightly toward the doorway.

"One more."

"How many patients need them."

"Three."

Jarvis averted his moist eyes away from the doctor as a flicker of apprehension tormented him. A crease of concern furrowed his brow. "Are they younger?"

"Yes."

Jarvis could see confusion and a merging impatience in the eyes that peered back at him over the mask. "He doesn't get it," he thought. Again, he asked, "Will I live?"

"Without the tube," the doctor finished brusquely. "No."

The man seems tired and frustrated, Jarvis thought. Suddenly he felt all alone, and scared. "I want my children." he mouthed.

"We're trying to reach them for you Mr. Heath," another, more comforting, almost sad voice replied. He felt a soft hand grasp one of his own and give a gentle squeeze. *Here is a kind soul who understands,* he thought.

Above him, the other, partially covered visage bore disapprovingly down. But then Jarvis saw it, an unexpected glint of insight, and a glaze of admiration. He could feel despair lift from his body and be replaced by decisive assurance. He knew his decision was the right one. "Let them live," Jarvis murmured slowly. "I've had a good life. My wife is waiting for me."

He had seen the patients lining the hall when he came in. On the few faces that were awake, he had recognized the desperation and fear he was feeling. *These people matter to someone, somewhere,* he thought.

"Mr. Heath."

"Yes. Sorry. Distracted." The words coming out slower than before.

"You want someone else to have your ventilator?"

"Yes."

"You're no ordinary man. You humble me."

"Thank you. Good life. I'm ready." he mumbled, probably too quiet for anyone to hear. With heroic effort, Jarvis stuck his thumb up.

"We'll make you comfortable. I promise" The doctor pulled aside one of the group and whispered some instructions, before leading the others out of the room.

He could see the kids' damp features as they did facetime with him. The nurse said family would not be allowed in the room but she would hold a phone in front of him so they could talk with each other. *Some technology I finally approve of,* Jarvis thought with a medley of visceral emotion.

"Hi kids," he murmured.

"Daddy, I love you," Shelly sputtered as tears cascaded down her cheeks.

Jarvis nodded slightly. He felt very tired, and breathing was harder. He could sense the wetness on his own cheeks.

"Dad, you're the best father we could ever have had. Love you," Michael whispered before turning away, and trying to hide his own flood of sadness. But his shoulders shook uncontrollably.

Jarvis nodded again, his face rigid with the effort to be strong for his children.

"Love you," he whispered gamely.

"This will help you rest Mr. Heath," a nurse said through her mask. He stared at the veil of moisture covering her eyes as she slowly injected some medicine into one of his IVs.

Jarvis barely nodded and hoped she could read minds. *I got to see my Michael and Shelley on the phone. Thank you. Love you kids. I'm coming Molly.* Then miraculously his lids became heavy, and despite a weak effort to breathe, he willingly surrendered to his body's plea to close his eyes.

Printed in the United States
by Baker & Taylor Publisher Services